BLUES & TRUE CONCUSSIONS

SIX NEW TORONTO POETS

To Michael & Lynn
Enjoy – best wishes
Edd
at Cheap Queers on Tallulah's
June 27/96

Selected and Introduced by Michael Redhill
Foreword by Dennis Lee
Afterword by Shawn Conway

To M+L —
Oh my toasty
treats!
love
R M Vaughan

Anansi

Published in 1996 by
House of Anansi Press Limited
1800 Steeles Avenue West
Concord, Ontario
L4K 2P3
Tel. (416) 445-3333
Fax (416) 445-5967

Canadian Cataloguing in Publication Data

Main entry under title:
Blues & true concussions

ISBN 0-88784-5819

1. Canadian poetry (English) — Ontario – Toronto.*
2. Canadian poetry (English) – 20th century.*
I. Redhill, Michael, 1966–   . II. Title: Blues and true concussions.

PS8259.7.T67B58 1996 C811'.5408'09713541 C96-930635-0
PR9198.3.T672B58 1996

Computer Graphics: Mary Bowness
Printed and bound in Canada

*House of Anansi Press gratefully acknowledges the support of the
Canada Council and the Ontario Arts Council in the development
of writing and publishing in Canada.*

CONTENTS

Christian Bök

R. M. Vaughan

Kevin Connolly

FOREWORD

BLUES & TRUE CONCUSSIONS belongs to a tradition of "debut" anthologies — collections that introduce emerging poets.

The editor of such an anthology makes a certain pact with the reader. Not that every poem will be a finished masterpiece. But that, providing the reader can discern the peers and titans a poet has been absorbing, each selection will reveal a thoughtful osmosis — and sometimes a leap ahead, toward the unknown poems the writer is making for. That's the greatest pleasure with a debut anthology: hearing the unmistakable *ping* as a gifted younger writer starts to speak in her own voice.

That process may seem inevitable in retrospect, when a poet has come fully into his own. But while you're sweating it through, there are no guarantees. In fact, it's a bitch. Speaking as one whose apprenticeship seemed to last forever, I'm moved by the particular sweat and accomplishments of each of the poets here.

There have been scores of debut anthologies in the century-plus of Canadian poetry. Some launch the editor and five of his friends, united mainly by the certainty that the literary establishment is set on excluding them. Others introduce poets with a commitment to socialism, say, or to the craft of Pound and Olson. Still others concentrate on new poets from one city or region. Some single out a few writers who have pretty much found their voices; others welcome a horde of beginners. But whatever its editorial rationale, each anthology will finally be assessed by a thing it can't include: the poetry its contributors go on to write.

Our best known debut collection is *New Provinces*, which in 1936 signalled the advent of modernism in English Canada. It presented Klein, Kennedy, Scott, and Smith of Montreal, Finch and Pratt from Toronto. Among the multitude of other anthologies, I think of Raymond Souster's *New Wave Canada*, which appeared in 1966. The last hurrah of Contact Press, it showcased seventeen young poets, including McFadden, Marlatt, nichol, Ondaatje, Wah. That was prescient enough. But Souster was omitting five poets whom he'd already published individually: Atwood, Bowering, Davey, MacEwen, and Newlove. Taken as a whole, that group debut may represent the greatest feat of talent scouting in our literature.

Of course the need to suss out new arrivals is perpetually renewed. Which leads to *Blues & True Concussions*.

This volume of new Toronto poets is published by Anansi. And thereby hangs a tale. When Dave Godfrey and I started the House of Anansi Press, several lifetimes ago in 1967, we had no idea what lay ahead. But within a year we were deluged with manuscripts, many too good to turn down.

So we started our own debut anthologies. The first, in 1968, was *T.O. Now: The Young Toronto Poets*. I recently borrowed a copy from Doug Fetherling (who was in the book himself), and sat down again with the thirteen poets I'd included. There they were, preserved in once-trendy sans serif — still assimilating the shockwaves of Dylan and Hendrix and dope, still pushing ahead from Ginsberg and Williams, Purdy and Ashbery. I found myself bemused by those brave beginnings. Why does one promising writer keep growing, I wondered, while five others bog down, drift away, burn out? I didn't know the answer . . .

That was T.O. then. What are gifted younger poets doing two artistic generations later? Is there an energy centre here now? And do these poets share any assumptions about mentors? or what a poem even *does*? Those were questions I wanted to explore when the Toronto Arts Foundation put one of its protegé awards at my disposal.

Fortunately, I had the good sense to take Michael Redhill as my guide. His *Lake Nora Arms* was one of the memorable arrivals of recent years. Now I discovered his openness to poets of many different persuasions. And as it turned out, that was the ideal approach; new poetry in Toronto comes in a neck-wrenching variety of idioms, which is part of why it's exhilarating. The project got lucky as well when Anansi went for it, with a commitment to new writers uncommon in larger houses. And so the wheel came full circle.

All that is throat-clearing, of course. What finally counts is the words on the page; that, and the poets themselves. It's boggling to see what dissimilar places they start from. In some, an antic intellectual energy is the long suit. In others it's the truths of the human heart. Some are hip as can be; others wouldn't know hip if it fell in their soup. And all are listening — but what different musics they hear!

Redhill gives us six men and women who are claimed by words. If you're like me, you'll want to see where that rendezvous leads them next.

— DENNIS LEE

INTRODUCTION

Toronto Then and Now

A book like this offers a pleasure usually afforded only by vacations and funerals: one is permitted to do some stock-taking, to stand back and make some shape out of a thing that by its proximity has only vague contours. Anthologists sometimes go berserk with this minor superpower and make oracular claims for what their books contain; I'll try to be more circumspect. I can't put forward any authority beyond my admiration for and interest in these poets. There were a couple of arbitrary but helpful parameters that limited the field — writers with one book or less; had to be Torontonians — but the main reason these poets are between these covers is that I love their work. Which is to say, I have no school to foment, no critical bone to pick.

The decision to select from poets who have published one book or less was a way of limiting the field to poets who have emerged from chrysalis, but haven't necessarily come to the general notice of readers. It isn't fair to call this a "generation" since these poets emerge from of many age-ranges and backgrounds, so I'll say "vintage." The previous crop have already fermented and had their chance to be utterly new, and must now be satisfied with being merely unknown. This book is meant to introduce a selection of promising writers who have moved into the press.

The Toronto part of this anthology has to do with its auspices. *Blues & True Concussions* was kicked off by Dennis Lee (from whose *Riffs* I've taken our title), via the Toronto Arts Foundation, who gave him its Lifetime Achievement Award last fall. A protegé award gave Lee the chance to create a project in his own community, hence this volume. All of this makes some synchronistic sense: Dennis Lee was the cofounder of Anansi, and he has been a force on the Toronto (as well as Canadian) literary scene since the late sixties.

So is Toronto still an "energy centre"? If there is a single major difference between the Toronto of *T.O. Now* and the present one, it's that a scattered scene has greatly cohered. The late sixties in Toronto was a time of putting down roots: Coach House Press, House of Anansi, and Rochdale were probably the most fertile soil, and thirty years later many of those shoots are still green. Writers who first appeared in that time remain active on today's literary scene, but have also become de facto mentors for the writers that followed them. Of these writers the most important for the poets of the last fifteen years are probably bp nichol, Michael Ondaatje, and Christopher Dewdney. The influence of these three poets is not restricted to the must-read category either; all three were teachers at one time or another at York University, and all three were active as editors at Coach House in the eighties. This is not to suggest that the writers in this book are under anyone's thrall, but rather that the Toronto of the eighties offered resources to the new writer that didn't exist even ten years earlier. A great number of writers who emerged in the late sixties have developed into mature voices in Toronto, and have remained here. It has transformed the city (and especially its universities) from a port to a capital of new writing. Just looking at the roster of teachers at York in the last fifteen years confirms this. In addition to nichol, Ondaatje, and Dewdney, younger writers have also encountered Lola Lemire Tostevin, Don Coles, Robert Casto, Fred Gaysek, Don Summerhayes, and Susan Swan at this, the epicentre of creative writing in eighties Toronto.

Another vector in the eighties was Toronto's vibrant small press scene. Spearheaded by such people as Victor Coleman and bp nichol, the small press community was a hive of publishing activity, and in this time some of the city's best-known independent publishers came into their own. They, in turn, encouraged a whole lawn's worth of grassroots writing. There were (and still are): j.w. curry's Curvd H&z, Maggie Helwig's Lowlife Publishing, Stuart Ross's Proper Tales Press, Nick Power's Gesture Press, Nicky Drumbolis's store and press, Letters, Kevin Connolly's Pink Dog, as well as Underwhich Editions, Streetcar Editions, and Contra Mundo Press, among other publishers and scads of little magazines. The community encouraged intense collegiality, an eclectic and wide range of publishing, as well as the obligatory rivalries and rifts.

The presence of writers in the universities and the anarchic publishing climate since the early eighties has meant that poets who began writing in this period had a genuine publishing and support infrastructure. The poets in this book, and their contemporaries, were lucky enough to have mentors and peers, but they have also had to struggle out from under the weight of such good fortune. In the Torontos of then and now it was always a battle to get your voice heard. Then it was seeking listeners, now it's making yourself audible over the din of influences and the activity of your peers. Poets who succeed in holding true to what sparked them in the first place find their way through this labryinth and plot poetic journeys of their own. The poets of *Blues & True Concussions* are out of the maze and very much on their way.

The Poets
Some of these six poets may be new to you, some may not. Their backgrounds are as diverse as their voices, and a fascinating array of tactics and intents inform their work. For the reader who doesn't want to wade in unattended, here's a brief primer on what turned one reader on to them.

Way back before it became extremely cool, I recall standing in the darkened main room of Bar Italia on College Street listening to **Eddy Yanofsky** read from his new book, *In Separate Rooms*. It was a crisp fall day, and as we listened to the poet's depictions of the city and the intimacy of kitchens, memories of a Montreal childhood and jazz-rooms, a kind of warm nostalgia overtook the room, even for the places that were right there, outside the door in the streets of our own city.

Yanofsky's work is shot through with the twin drives of sadness and pleasure, and they have always been poems for me that expose, in a seemingly simple way, the emotional roots of place. Yanofsky, a transplanted Montrealer, is a city poet in the tradition of Souster and Layton, and the presence of the city in Yanofsky's poems is not only as a character or a backdrop, but also as the site of a subjective reality, complicated by the poet's reactive glance. So the speaker in "The Gap" observes a city commonplace — a person covered by blankets in a doorway — and slips with no apparent transition to the internalization of his reaction. Yanofsky doesn't turn away and weep (à la Layton), but wants, suddenly, to kick the hell out of anything in his way. Here, there is no larger moral agenda: the voice in Yanofsky's poetry is frequently so overwhelmed by what it sees that it's only possible to react. In "Two Days to January," he writes of a "dysfunction in the brain" and his inability to stave off the "unwilled reunions" a walk in the city provokes. This is a voice utterly joined to the life of the city. Yanofsky does not stand back and pontificate, he draws you in to the streets and voices with him.

In other poems, Yanofsky is the lover looking back on love, or the grown man looking back on rude health. In poems like "Solarium" and "Chai," he captures in gently persuasive lyrics the hope of ongoing life and love, and these are poems that offer the reader incomplete solace with a kind of graciousness that is rare to uncover among new poets.

In **Laura Lush**'s work, the reader at first encounters a façade of narrative convention, but then quickly discovers a poetry charged with a private cosmology, the elements of which are in a state of constant transformation. In these poems, an image-alphabet recurs with obsessive regularity, like the cards in a tarot deck, each time ordered differently, emphasizing different aspects of a secret life. We are visited again and again in Lush's poetry with the spirits of the moth, the wolf, stars, the moon, opals, fish, mushrooms, plums, oranges, berries, worms, and skin of every sort.

Sometimes Lush has the eye of a camera, moving inexorably closer to her subject until the detail that has gripped her is fully exposed to us. Frequently we are horrorstruck, but always the world seems to have been reinvented in these poems. In "Jessie," we are witness to a woman showing her cancerous lumps to the curious "we" of the poem. Lush depicts the woman's cancer in context of the warmth and fullness of summer; a peach tree that hangs on tight to its fruit. And then, like Jessie shaking the tree for its fruit, cancer takes "parts of her away, / summer casting its gold lures." Such moments of breathless innovation are general in Lush's poetry. Worms in a bed of soil are "like coins in a chocolate cake," and elsewhere, the moon is transformed into a wolf: "a brilliant blue flame / through the trees."

At other times, however, Lush's gaze is more unwavering, and what opens before our eyes surprises us with sudden holiness. Sometimes it's the shocking numinous of Plath, at other times a more simply stated spirituality, like that of Brodsky or Milosz. When we read "The dark / lopes back home. / My mother cave comes / clean," we know something unusual is going on, we know a secret has been told, a singular myth has been cracked open. The promise of this kind of poetry is to enlarge us. And it does, as it also enlarges the world written of. Lush instructs the moon to rub its "mint throat across deer" and you know damn well it will.

The first poem I ever saw by **Christian Bök** was "Diamonds." (Four of its fourteen parts are reprinted here.) What struck me about this poem was how it seemed to be happening all over the page all at once. The pages of this poem not only refract the memory of a gem-cutting father, but its shape mimics the facets of a gem. Little squares of text brighten here and there, their contents capturing thought and reflecting it back.

When his book *Crystallography* came out, the full extent of Bök's talent was revealed. This collection moved with ease between modes as different as lyrical poetry and pataphysics. Some poems, like "Grain Boundaries," seemed to reference the sound poetry of the seventies (and hearing Bök read this poem in increasingly faster cycles only confirmed this), but the poem on the page innovates, taking an almost static linear form, though it explodes into tumbling phonemes even when read silently. In other places, an apparently rigorous scientific mode takes over. The atomic structure of gems (such as "Emerald") is represented in a tangle of gridded elemental compounds, but below the crystalline structures, Bök has used the first letter of each element to decode the secret life of the gem.

Aligned with artists as diverse as Chris Dewdney and Kurt Schwitters, Bök is nonetheless blazing trails into unmarked territory. His "univocalic" novel-in-progress entitled *Eunoia* goes places only Georges Perec would dare. Each chapter of the novel employs but a single vowel, and as the reader will see from the selections printed here, the tactic, which may seem merely playful at first, asserts through repetition an actual personality to the vowel in use. These three chapters use the letter "a," and this letter, sentry to the entire alphabet, is revealed to be hip, energetic, a little jittery and very funny.

R. M. Vaughan's poetry is one primarily of unstopped emotion. His poems deliberately obliterate the line between the personal and political and do it with a kind of reckless grace: this is a dervish poetry, which scatters itself on the page and demands you adapt yourself to its energies. When he reins in, as in the poems from "Sickness Lexicon" or the "Bed Poems," you can feel the tension provoked by Vaughan's restraint. The effect is one of a roiling under-surface, and the reader finds in these poems a form that intimates the end-spectrum emotions of Vaughan's poetry: ecstasy and grief.

In keeping with the brio of such a poetry, Vaughan's lines and image-patterns stay in a state of constant synaptic disruption. In the fifth section of "Sickness Lexicon," the poet writes of the despair of sickness, and between his own lines appear Baudelaire's invoking the terrors of *l'irrésistible Nuit*. Almost everywhere else, Vaughan's poetry is subject to the eruptions of parenthetical thoughts, emergences from the sub-subconsciousness of the poems: the doubts, second-guessings, editorial commentaries, and alternate views that other poets may leave out for the sake of fomenting an authoritative voice. Vaughan's work courageously exposes its cognitive layers, defying the reader's desire for closure.

In "The World of Ice," Vaughan exposes the homoerotic subtext of the sea-faring adventure story, relentlessly playing and punning in his subject's chosen idioms ("Our Hero buried deep in the stern") until the stale metaphors are released to new life. But his motive isn't always revision: in the selection from his "Bed Poems," the remasking impulse is directed at a reclamation of the erotic: these are straightforward and ecstatic poems of sexual love, perhaps not unusual in themselves, but rare now among gay poets for their unbridled and griefless carnality. As in all of Vaughan, they are a vivid warrant of love and loss, hope and anger.

Kevin Connolly's poetry states an immediate argument against itself. This is poetry contra poetry, a largess of language about diminishing returns; complete gestures intimating incomplete things. Here, "a world resigns itself to shallow desperation." Using a broad range of tactics from dadaist cut-ups to poems developed from titles to seeming absurdism, Connolly canvasses suspicion and giddy angst for openings into "the real." But what comes across at first as the apparently random coalesces into sobering order. He is "not articulate but . . . that other thing," and later in the same poem discovers, to the calmest horror imaginable, that things are "not nearly so wild or / impressive as I had hoped."

In Connolly's work, fragments of things remembered and imagined (no distinction seems to be made) jockey for semantic status as they clatter down around the poet's head. Amazing locutions are forged, sudden discourses are revealed. The whip-smart language rips open intellectual wormholes, and cliché and barb sleep together in the same stanza: "We'll argue till the cows come home," Connolly writes, and then goes to town with our brains: "dragging their fart-produced ozone holes / like an October tailwind / hauls a Goodyear Blimp / the 'Step Smartly' of Akron, Ohio."

After this, the reader may expect a cornucopia of hilarity and fetching insights, but Connolly's work sells you a ticket for the stand-up act and leaves you in your seat for the end of the world. "Things aren't nearly / as ornate as they pretend to be," he warns us, and promises punishment for those "whose faces / brighten before the answer is given." Connolly's is a loaded poetry, but its trigger sets something off in the reader, a small explosion in the brain that insists all is not what it seems.

Only four years ago, I recall reading **Esta Spalding**'s first poems, and seeing in them the burgeonings of a talent that has matured astonishingly fast. Drawing sometimes on a Hawaiian past, sometimes on the figures of friends and loved ones, this is an intimate poetry that reveals rich ties to places and people, and that, taken as a whole, is the record of a passionate witness.

Chief among the spells cast in Spalding's poetry is the way what is held or seen or heard heralds the appearance of lost things. A gift of ginger blossoms in "When the Box Arrived" triggers "hibiscus, bougainvillea, bird / of paradise" in a locale and time far from the present. But the evocation of other times and places is merely nostalgiac if it isn't paired with another purpose, and Spalding twins emotional archaeology to the politics of remembering. In her most recent work, the world insists itself more pointedly, the act of recalling or telling becomes more diffi-cult, if only because it is also the profession of history-writers, war-mongers, and strike-breakers. Here, the poet admonishes herself to hold to things that have "not quite been / forgotten" and to carefully reassemble them, since the tectonic shifting of memory provides only fragments.

The lushness of these fragments, however, is what imbues

Spalding's poetry with its particular abundance and vitality. The irony of these poems about skeletal things (like memory) is how generous they are, how fleshed with the natural and inner worlds. Here we are compelled to partake of red wine, running deer, dogfish, salt, a lover's spine, and "supple bodies before the tanks." A lightning-rod for things sensual, Spalding captures everything around her and sets it down, sparking it with a luminous intelligence and lending it a private grace.

A Benevolent Flame

When Dennis Lee began publishing his seminal anthologies of poetry at House of Anansi Press in the sixties and seventies, what he was doing, above all, was acting out his faith in a good enterprise. Some of the dividends of his work can be seen here: a generation of new poets and editors who have footsteps to follow in. I am grateful to Dennis Lee for asking me to collect these poets, and to Anansi — old and new — for being the keeper of a benevolent flame.

— MICHAEL REDHILL
Toronto, March 1996

EDDY YANOFSKY

. . . the peace I was desiring . . .

Solarium

1

This is like the top deck
of a ship at night,
the buoyancy of reflections,
traffic navigating the universe
and far away—
the Cartier Bridge
the Champlain Bridge,
lights connecting Montreal,
the island, and its south shore.
Roman candles,
a phospherous helplessness,
a hanging permanence that
can't be extinguished.

2

Wind blows through the pines
down Mount Royal
hums like a generator in a glass chamber,
stirs snow and coattails,
suspends traffic where it converges
at Cedar and Pine
looking like white unblemished tracks
in a Laurentian pastoral.

3

I loop the belt of my terry cloth robe
around my palm like worry beads,
press against the radiator plate,
run my fingers across its vent
until I have a bees nest under control.

Where has appetite gone? Had I ever known
it? Is it hunger, or the disease?

The sensation from the tenth floor solarium
is pure height,
like the catwalk above the logo of the Canadiens
at the Montreal Forum.
Only I'm watching hockey in the seminary skating rink below,
the rattle of sticks are really test tubes,
my bruised arms are not from
yesterday's game.
I can pretend that here the world exists
on three sides of this room,
the city spreading out from the Montreal General Hospital
like a formidable moat.

4

All I smell
is steamed halibut.
The only sea smell.
The sanctuary of the solarium
is no exception.
It's everything that is wrong
about healing, it's
the pit in my stomach
or the inflammation.
The inescapable end of the hallway.
The west side of the solarium looking
onto the belle epoch high rise
that owns the horizon, burns its lights
to simulate ships in port,
(impossible to see
for the grain elevators
and the limitations of
windows at night).
A glare from the EXIT sign
shadows the form of a terrycloth robe,
and a hospital I.D. bracelet
hovers like a halo
over Place Ville Marie.

Two Days to January

His day progressed
into journeys:

the unwilled reunions
as he walked the back lanes
where he liked to think
he didn't have to think —

the long attention to a bird
turning its head,
open beak offering the metallic
whine of a saw blade bending.

His complex associations after
a red car drove past with all of
its windows smashed, the driver
plucking shards as only
an accident victim who is
an aesthete can do — one hand
on the wheel, the other fussing.

He puzzled over distances in his mind,
the mercantile details of where he would
descend for New Year's shopping.

He tried to piece together the broken glass
of the red car into perfect windows where
he would have seen his own reflection
at 30 mph; a figure stunned by the incongruous
bundle of winter clothing; his quilted hat like
Chinese and Russian soldiers wear when
posing for still life propaganda photos in *Time*.

He saw a young man on folded legs
out of the cold in the Bay subway station,
proprietor of the tiled wall. He took particular
note of his worn ski jacket, a Boston Bruins
toque and pants of no distinction other
than smears, a sign on the tiled wall,
"Lost Articles." He wondered if the young
man chose his spot to be ironic,

reasoned suddenly that cold wars are
strictly personal, humanity distanced
from a conventional process of peace —
a collective incapacity to order our lives
for the "moment."

It made him think of the cold
wars he had been incapable of resolving;
a dysfunction in the brain.

Coat Buttons

1.

If you sing soft music
to your foetus
If you whisper mathematics

lying in bed waiting:

how to
raise a child who will
do well in science
and art.

2.

The child I see this
pregnant woman carry
will not complain about
the cold wind's teeth,
a snapping turtle fossilized
in ice.

Her coat has two middle
buttons open and still, it
stretches over her

belly stretches over the child
who will be called names by
children of other races

who will be born
under a winter sign

who will love
a cold wind,
sing its chorus from
memory,
know its velocity by
instinct.

July

The air in the park off
St. Clair Avenue —
a child herds pigeons on the grass
who only see her
checkered leotards
and knees coming at them
like pistons.

Maybe her arms waving
is what stops them
as I keep going
down into the subway
where these places
all smell the same
once you've been there —

Toronto, Paris, London.
Concrete containing water
that sweeps out of lakes

and swells in toilets, returns to rivers,
evaporates into the atmosphere,

regenerates into our memories.

The Gap

What are doors for anyway
if not for soiled bed comforters
piled in heaps?

The quilted comforter I almost kicked
lay in front of the green doors
that opened for an evangelical event
at Varsity Stadium last summer.

After it rained, snow appeared;
one fat flake after another,
so slowly
I could have used them
for batting practice.

I wanted to kick anything in my way.
Even the stadium looked like an overripe sternum
to punch the lights out of.

There were legs under the comforter,
just shin bones attached to
a body without gender,

suede Wallabees nobody wears anymore.

Spit

Clotted white pools
on the sidewalk
from Spadina to Euclid Avenue —
the liquid of fifty-seven
distinct libretti.

Their chorus to which we danced
made us think of notation
that had to land somewhere —
the sound of the bass clef
rising up through the treble clef,
throats clearing
whole notes, half notes
triplets splattering.

Like folk dancers
we jumped in spasms:

to the salsa of boom boxes,
to the minor keys of Asia,
to the percussion of clogs.

Fragments from the Survival Journal of a
  Euclid Avenue Resident in the Wilderness

I have a burning urge to pee
on Highway 400,
frost bitten feet
in Ben's Landtrooper, me
the untrooper in the rear seat.

Mary's cheeks are flushed
the colour of her
shiny parka skin,
not the skin I covered her with

last night
when we talked
of her Druid roots

in tree limbs
starlings cover off the 400, now
teaming into wilderness-like-stuff,

wilder-weariness setting in.
    "hug a tree!"
no, I want to hug
the concrete underpass
and reach back
to pull the highway
(conduit to the city)
the way I would drag
my blanket from room

to room as a child.
And I try to keep myself from asking her
what kind of birds are those, and those,

starling clouds which blacken geometrically,
Escher's patch of muted sky,
singed here and there

November, a short drive
back to the city. But the wheels
keep rolling northward,
beyond the exit for
Penetanguishene

a name sounded out for the first time
like wild rice,
soft and coarse in the mouth.

Indeterminate

We were in the dairy aisle,
shadows under our eyes,
at least three of us,
staring at lumps of cheddar
wrapped in cellophane,
their identical price stickers.
The white porcelain refrigerator
made me want to sleep. It was
like viewing a corpse: the epitome
of the peace I was desiring.

The others crowded around so
I reached into the folds
of their winter coats, as if my arm
was a strand of something, a fibre
loosed from the cold white bed.

They moved apart for me
with consideration for the living.

I realized I'd forgotten about
the birth certificate for my mortgage signing,
right then
paying for my cheddar, with
snow flakes holding
against the supermarket window
like clusters of tombstones.

Then that indeterminate feeling
of being kept alive for something:
the cashier waving a wand across
the magnetic stripe of my credit card,
a pause, an affirmative
bleat.

Sestina for a Place

The Bretonne figures of a man and a woman
stand in a tulip patch on the coffee bowl
we gave each other in Montreal
A blue glazed sky circles the lip
above the Bretonnes' head gear. There another patch
of small carrots and a purple radish

fill the bowl placed next to the giant radish
on the window sill, a surprise for the woman
I live with occasionally. Her plan is to make us bowls
for soup in her ceramics studio in Montreal,
although one does not exist yet, and the way of her
    trembling lip
when I upset things makes me tremble and desperate to patch

the cracks in our relationship, like the patches
of topsoil filling the cracks of the giant radish.
I found it in November, a knotted root like the elderly woman
with arthritic hands who dips them in a bowl
of dried petals from the flower sanctuary overlooking Montreal.
Her tongue traces her lower lip

washing away the colour and flavour of her rose lip-
stick, concentrating on her impressionist patch
of reconstructed flowers. It will be a gift for our new Montreal
apartment, which does not exist yet, a woman
and I will share, more than occasionally, near the lawn bowl
club in Westmount. There, the roots of a culture, like the
    giant radish

I found in my garden in November, flourish somehow, with
    sealed lips
as if a dress code is sufficient expression. But the green patch
of lawn, even as moss, will face the kitchen we may have in
    Montreal
by next spring, in time for Passover and horseradish,
ritual seder with family and friends the woman
I occasionally live with won't know. But their bowls

of soup will have been her invention, the glazed lips
inviting an elderly aunt to raise her bowl
revealing a seaweed patch
which will sway in the current of the soup in Montreal,
an illusion created in her studio which does not exist yet, like
    the radish
which appeared in my garden in November I surprised the
    woman

I occasionally live with, the woman who is learning to make
    bowls
for salads of radicchio in the Montreal
kitchen we may have in the spring, maybe.

The Meadow and Breeze

Sunflowers facing the morning,
old curled petals
weighing on bent
stalks taller than me
reach out
as if to hear my neighbour's parents
speaking German.

Vines with purple trumpets
and green spade pads
poke through the fence
where city slugs have turned the radish greens
into the cut-out snowflakes of
my childhood.

Mary's old pedal bike
sits upside down,
one wheel at the repair shop
the other spinning in the breeze
like a windmill sail
disguising purpose with creaking grace.

And I am lucky we have
no purpose among the wildflowers,
the dishevelled, unkempt lawn,
and radio voices across the fence.

We imagine
the kick-stand,
dismantled fom her bike,
is a Picasso bull.

Serpentine Road

We both heard the noise on the roof.
A Buddhist gong resonating
through the building's plumbing,
me trying to visualize
Serpentine Road in Bermuda
and her dreaming she's
one of Shakespeare's witches
back from a weekend in the north
with two other women.
It's something frightening and peculiar to her,
adding to my fears
because I might have that dream
and haven't read Macbeth.

If only the cats would lie still
but they too sense
this sudden change in the room —
a crescent moon in the south
that hasn't shifted to the west,
so unusual this close to dawn
that we embrace and change
the geography of their sleep —
our feet shifting under the covers.

We're a bit crazy,
change this mood with
light from my lamp.
Then I think how the wind
bangs the storm shutters
on my sister's house,
when it's wild at night
blowing away the sound of tree frogs
that chirp like hatched eggs,

the only way in which I can justify
my fear of them; imagine their multitudes
flinging off branches and fronds,
tiny buds scattered across the road
pebbling the ride under the moped.

I could hear the storm shutters
bang like crazy from Serpentine Road,
past the narrow roundabout
where the roads cut thin as cross-hairs,
where lights are on
in limestone buildings
and someone slams a screen door.
This was before my wife,
when it was impossible
to imagine my sister sleeping soundly
in the gale winds on that island.

Now I release the beaded lamp cord.
The roof bangs
and I tell both of us;
it's the plumbing, what else?
let's stop scaring ourselves.
But she's already calm.
I lie back,
watch our windows,
the moon, and wait
for other lights.

Chai
(for Micky Absil)

I've only seen a photograph —
boats anchored on the muddy shoals
of the Ganges. Splintered canopies
on top of blistered bows and sterns,
sari'd women leaving their men
to wash, or launch the dead
among the reeds.

A shadow surfaces
of a passing nimbus
that could be a pod of something.

I've been taking my tea brewed with
cardamon and milk: olive green
pods half submerged in coppery liquid.
Stirred, it raises the silt
of the river, spreads the aromatics of
ceremony, produces the sensation
that life will be remembered.

Figures

We have ritual love
when the full moon apes
the skating pond
beside the deep pitch
of Lake Ontario.

Passenger jets
on the same arcing flight
cut figures across the reflection of ice
and frozen air currents
penetrate our bedroom
with surgical exactness.

We live in this world of
delineated space —
the full moon crosses
the bluntness of our bodies.

LAURA LUSH

The dark lopes back home . . .

The First Awakening of Summer

In the riverbed, a fish, ruby bright
startles a rock to life.
Trees bend their million buds
popping like corks.
Happy, the moon goes on and on
about plums.

The Other Side of the Lake

Frank and Bea Donkersley lived on the other side,
the sandy part where their dock jutted
out in a long brown tongue.
Around their cottage were the birches
and the laugh lines of sun at dusk.
Our cottage was on the rocky side — a chocolate
melted into marble.
Every morning our father would throw us off the dock
emptying that two room cottage
like you'd empty a fishbowl.
On the other side we could see Frank and Bea
sitting at the dock's edge sipping coffee,
Frank's hairy chest like a blanket of spiders.
In the afternoon, we'd beg them to take us over,
our orange motor boat plotting through the water.
When we got there Frank would stand up and salute us
with his tall gin, in his plaid bathing suit, the white
peaked cap. Then he'd walk over and say, "Fee, Fie, Fo, Fum,"
cup his giant hands over our pink-shell ears,
lift us up as if lifting us from the earth we'd been planted
in for a little while, the slender parsnips of our bodies
dangling so we could see his face —
those wonderful fuzz-covered ears creeping open.

This Farm Where Nothing Sleeps and Nothing Is Invisible

Some old man's last tractor load shrinking
round the gums of the white picket fence.
The blue-tick hound covered in burrs —
a gas pump rusted tight,
the horse-licked cube of salt
whittled to a speck.
The corner of the shed that leaks rats,
grease roasting in the grooves of saddles.
And those ageing cats, blisters of hot tar in noon's sun
waiting for the cultivator to
peel back field mice.

The Worm Girl

I am the Worm Girl.
I drive a Wonderbread truck,
converted — good tires,
bumpers black as jujubes.
Every weekend I drive the Grey Bruce County,
all the silvered lakes,
birches waving like old drunks.
In back I have 25,000 worms
deep in earth
like coins in a chocolate cake.
Sometimes they wriggle to the top,
luminous as half-moons,
their skins onion-blue.
What they feel is my hand,
each finger a lure
urging them gently out
like a carrot's midwife.
I reward them with light.

The Missing Child

After porridge, CFRB — Jocko Thomas
reporting from police headquarters —
my brother, sister, and I would walk
out of our white house, cutouts
strung together by our common flesh,
our metal lunchpails clanging back and forth.
Then her name on the radio six times a day
while the teachers skulked around the playground,
dragging their arms like sad chimpanzees.
We all bunched together — the blonde, brown,
black caps of sticky hair. Cluster of suckers.
Our mothers walked us to the bottom
of driveways, waited until the orange school bus
appeared, sent us out on invisible lines
attached to their eyes. But she had
gotten into that big blue sedan
slipping quick as a moth through
the crack in a door.

In the Bus Depot

In the bus depot, the girl
wearing the stray cardigan
leans against the photo booth
waiting for her pictures
to slide out of the machine.
Every five seconds, the humping
lights, the processor eating
her smile. She remembers earlier —
the sun sliding in and out
of her shirt like a warm foreign
lover. She doesn't move, preferring
to stand like a tall cold elm,
running her fingernails up and down
her pant zipper. When the photos slide
out, they smell of blue gum and sun
on the pavement at noon. She doesn't
want to look at them all at once,
or too soon, so she walks into the bathroom,
the curl of her fresh photos wagging
from her palm. In the stall, she examines
the poses that range from serious to comic.
Sometimes the lips mocking the eyes
or vice versa. She will send one
to her boyfriend, one to her cousin
in the next town, and one to her mother
when she discovers her missing.

Jessie

We'd sit around her lawnchair
while the wet butts of Rothmans
spread like mushrooms through
the grass. "Here, feel these,"
she'd say, lifting up
her arms to reveal the two
peach pits on either side
of her breasts. "Hard as rocks."
That summer, the fruit clung
desperate as men overboard.
And Jessie under the tree
shaking the low tentacles of branches,
a sound like slow hail.
Baskets filled with the deep
June fragrance while the cancer
mapped its lubricious path,
taking parts of her away,
summer casting its gold lures.

157 Islington

When you open the door garlic blooms like roses,
a pudding of stale air in the hallway.
Leszek is making dinner, his face scorched red from vodka.
Tomorrow he'll start English classes — he can feel
the words in his mouth exquisite as mints.
In another room is the one who sat in prison,
the sad numb vegetables of his hands.
He's been here the longest, he's seen seasons collide.
Everyday he watches the light under his
door scuttle like mice.

In the Puszcza

In the secret forest mushrooms glow
in velvet stupors. Under moss,
skulls whiten like well-kept streetlamps,
empty conchs were you to hold them to your ears.
Yet the deer, the lynx, and boar live on freely,
nudging at still-uncovered helmets.
The night's shiny as a cut.
And sometimes they find them, face down —
skeletons with the dainty bracelets
of barbed wire round their angel-thin bones.

Note: *Puszcza* is Polish for forest.

After the Monsoon

They are fishing in the river,
the lemon-bruise of the monsoon
still swollen on the banks.
The quick slice of lines and
sun snapping through trees.
The girls kneel on the banks,
their skirts tight between their legs,
mindful of their fathers' catches —
the fat slap of fish on tables,
knives opening up all the blue-hooked deaths.
When the river finally slows,
the flecked fins rise,
turn in the cool mud
as the banks breathe in and out with fish.
It's the first time in months anything
has broken the surface.

When They Go

Fall loosens
a canopy of geese.
The slow drifts of honking.

Already November and a few of them
are by the baseball field.
Their whiteness leavens the acres
of brick-smudged houses.

These are the phoenix mornings
when the sky rises with wings.

And the one in front,
tilling through fog.
I wave him on, "Go! Go!"

Stars

The stars appear one by one
like small songs,
like small terrors
rattling bright in their cages.
The moon so skin.
Pale rice paper
awash in blood.

The wolf —
a brilliant blue flame
through the trees.

Summer

Between the rows of corn, the gold pronouncements
of summer, the earth is scarred by our backs.

Tiny vagrants alone in our bodies.
Mottled children who have strayed from our homes.

Nothing insurmountable — the warm wet passageway
to the underground fort.

On either side, the earth moving its cow belly.
Slow song of grass yellowing.

The boys' crude beds of stones and twigs. Pyres
we later sink into the ground.

All of this to keep us away from the small pouch of marbles —
the limed eyes of birds glowing off sticks.

All things transfixed:
the chrysalides' luminous quiet, the stars' rubied prayers.

De-winged, leaves jostling across the sky.

What's left?

Our bodies, the axis under the weight of copper sky.
Our belief that all things begin from our hands,

that even summer can be contained in a jar —
that one butterfly bright enough to last past autumn.

As our heads keep turning with the blue curve of earth,
pulling legs, arms toward the fantastic rush of our lives.

This Wound Is a Flower
a cycle of poems

It is possible that there is no other memory than the memory of wounds.
— Czeslaw Milosz, Nobel Prize Lecture, 1980

I. SPRING

It is April and the small-bodied cherries
cling to the trees like suicide attempts.
Just the same, the couples are in love
and quite unaware of these.
They only see the sky wide and opening,
the flowing stitches of birds.

II. VENGEANCE

An olive drops from a branch.
Peacefully,
the river assembles —
a current swallowing a stone.
But a single olive
thrown from a hand —
is enough to shatter
all the star-laid lakes.

III. SAMARITAN

I carried you that night,
even though your body wasn't in my arms.
Instead — a hovering, a mothed knife
flitting around my wrists.
While she — the dark-eyed one — gave you tea,
stitched you — thread by thread — shut.

IV. LOVER

As you lay in bed,
your body floated above
the talk of lilies.
Girls, drunkenly, called your name.
I peeled your shadow from you,
wrapped it around my body.
Like a lover.
Like love's hot poultice.

V. MOTHER CAVE

The dark
lopes back home.
My mother cave comes
clean. Spooled tight, bone
flaying bone. You fold into me.
Difficult origami
with your steel-honed wings.

VI. BENEDICTION

When you turned on the light
the blood like a poppy
under your nose.
Above, that one gecko —
a blue vein on the ceiling.
Even more remarkable:
the night — like all the evil
gathering before song.

VII. DESCENT

After, everyone wanted
to know what happened.
Especially the children
with their night-bereft eyes.
They held candles up to your face,
watched your irises eat
their small tails of fear.

VIII. RENEWAL

Listen,
if I could make
you see colour, you would rise
again like a beautiful
spring crocus.
You would unpin
your arms from the sky,
suck the small holes
in your hands
until the wounds
hissed warm.
You would drink cup after
cup of sweet milk
mistake it for my own.
If I could make
you see colour, you would pluck
your own heart,
peel it like a plum.
And taste and taste.

Blue

If I had to do it again,
I would forgive you
without a second thought.
And in forgiving you
I would forgive
all the others —
those who vanished
into jungles, the dark crevices
of night.

I would bite
my own umbilical cord.
I would stop the rivers
of mother
in my own body.

I would wrestle
the seed
under —
its conifer head
splitting.

I would spit out all
the faulty wires,
the chipped
genes.

I would remove
my heart,
return
it to the wolf.

Opal Moon

Opal moon,
beatific moon.

Bigamist among
the shuddering stars.

Carry this old earth,
cradle the lakes and trees.

Rub your mint throat across deer.

Come quickly, come quietly,
the animals are retreating.

The fox, the hare, the speckled bands
of snakes. Slowly, slowly,
undulating south.

The Ravine

We are nine and ten,
tiny brush strokes of legs,
arms that have just unwrapped
the world for the first time.

Down to the ravine
past the innocuous stench of winter,
the trees locked in their
death-scents

we run past
the numbed buds of trees
the white mouths of icicles
shiny as fish.

We see the white houses
that brick our dreams every night.
The unflowing river.
How its water has stopped for us,
hardened like our brothers' penises.
With our skateblades
we unstitch the ice,
split the pond's
underbelly.

We are girls
so we wait for blood
while our mothers
swell in their ageing pods.

The first snow
falls blackly, darkly.

We hook our young bodies
into the cold, into each other

while two dogs entwine.
The thick bud where their bodies meet.

The female always pulls away first,
the neck hair raised, the back legs
the most vulnerable of bows.

Toward the pond she runs as we hold the male back
by the scruff —
their history a brief flash of snow.

We wait for her soft-padded retreat —
the long thin blade of her bark
that signals she's safe.

CHRISTIAN BÖK

. . . ethereal celestina . . .

Crystals

A crystal is an atomic tessellation, a tridimensional
jigsaw-puzzle in which every piece is the same shape.

A crystal assembles itself out of its own constituent
disarray: the puzzle puts itself together, each piece
falling as though by chance into its correct location.

> A crystal is nothing more
> than a breeze blowing sand
> into the form of a castle
> or a film played backwards
> of a window being smashed.

A compound (word) dissolved in a liquid
supercooled under microgravitational
conditions precipitates out of solution
in (alphabetical) order to form crystals
whose structuralistic perfection rivals
the beauty of machine-tooled objects.

An archaeologist without any mineralogical
experience
might easily mistake a crystal
for the artificial product of a precision
technology.

A word is a bit of crystal in formation.

Crystal Lattice

```
  c     l
crystal        c     l
  y     t    crystal        c     l
  s  lattice  y     t    crystal
  t  a  i       s  lattice  y     t
lattice        t  a  i       s  lattice
  l  t  e  c    lattice        t  a  i
     i  crystal t  e  c    lattice
     c     y     t  i    crystal t  e
     e     s  lattice  y     t  i
           t  a  i  e     s  lattice
     c     lattice        t  a  i  e
crystal t  e  c    lattice
  y     t  i    crystal t  e  c     l
  s  lattice  y     t  i    crystal
  t  a  i  e     s  lattice  y     t
lattice        t  a  i  e     s  lattice
  l  t  e  c    lattice        t  a  i
     i  crystal t  e  c    lattice
     c     y     t  i    crystal t  e
     e     s  lattice  y     t  i
           t  a  i  e     s  lattice
     c     lattice        t  a  i  e
crystal t  e  c    lattice
  y     t  i    crystal t  e  c     l
  s  lattice  y     t  i    crystal
  t  a  i  e     s  lattice  y     t
lattice        t  a  i  e     s  lattice
  l  t  e       lattice        t  a  i
     i          l  t  e       lattice
     c          i             l  t  e
     e          c                i
                e                c
                                 e
```

FIGURE 2.1: A goniometric device for measuring
the interfacial angles of a crystal.

Turbulent winds can break off the fragile branches of a stellar
crystal as it falls, and often the branches regenerate themselves
during the descent, but even after reaching the ground these snow
fragments are still not free from modification: winds continue
to disintegrate each crystal by abrading it against other crystals
so that, when the fallen remnant comes to rest at last beneath
the microscope of the observer, the specimen often bears little
resemblance to the original particle formed high in the ionosphere.

Emerald

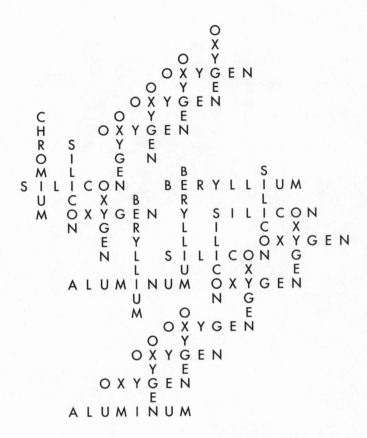

crownland beaumontage:

sidereal
opulence of sinfulness.

opaque, ornate, orphic.

silkscreens of silent
orchards.

oracular silviculture.

alembic of silhouettes:

bezels,
oblique optics.

berylloid observatory.

alkali,
octane, oxides.

ozone overworld of oz.

from **Diamonds**
for Carl Johnston

1)

C is for diamond

the one gem   my father
                       was a sad
made of one   gemcutter

element: carbon

                          he made jewels more precious
chimney soot   by smashing them, spoke only
crushed coal   words pared down to the edge
charred wood   of their silence, and strove

fire at its core   to break into (break out of)

                            each house
                            of mirrors

                         held at the tip of his tongs

my father   he retired, nerves
taught me   shot by the threat
precision   of a slipped razor

2)

a diamond is   transparent charcoal:

 a darkness
 so intense   under pressure
                                all things are
the eye sees   clear, just be

   through it   sure you
                                        remember

my father once   diamond dust is black
gave me a gift

an apache tear
a black pebble

opaque till you held it   after hours of solitude
up against direct light   when drunk, he recalled

then the smoke   the native widow
trapped inside   who lamented her
became visible   loss for so long
                                        the great spirit
                                        transfigured her
                                        tears into drops
       my father   of black crystal
       too broke   thus bequeathing
       to be wed
       never got   to all who fall in love
       my mother   keepsakes of her sorrow
       a diamond

       he claimed to adore her
       too much to profane her
       with gems made of ashes

52

3)

blowtorch   organic stone
a diamond
                                       not sterile
                                       but burning

                                   crystals made

enkindled
when ruby   from the same
                                   thing as life

it blazes   *abcdefghijklmnopqrstuvwxyz*

just as   my father opened the field
melting   guide to crystals to pages
dry ice   with fine print to show me
                                   how to decipher a language

vaporizes
                                   he gave me his gemcutter's
                                   eyepiece and left me alone
                                   to revel in detail: edges
                                   of serifs, fibres in paper

as breath
                                   only later did he teach me
                                   how to sound out the words

LIFE: the percentage of light that a diamond
      reflects back towards its viewer

FIRE: the degree to which a diamond refracts
      light into its component colours

LIFE X FIRE = BRILLIANCE: (all this is true)

4)

plato was
the first
to regard

he studied
mineralogy
at antwerp

a diamond as
frozen quintessence

a soul in   my father   tended saw   saw
suspended   taught me   for a firm   one
animation   precision   in brücken   gem

a vestige of heaven   take two
within earth   years to
                                                   be split
                                                   into two

all his life an attempt

to see the free point
trapped in perfection

dei mundi

my father
put faith
in no god

Glass

Mercurial magma

sand,
lime, and soda
            cool
into a vitreous
solid,
the most viscous
            fluid,

a virtual liquid
thick
enough to seem
            rigid:

fragile language.

Glass represents
a poetic element

exiled
to a borderline

between
states of matter:

breakable water
not yet frozen,
yet unpourable.

Chatoyant panes

  in cathedral
  windows flow

too slow
for eyes to see

  illuminated
  manuscripts

written
on glass pages

bleeding away
ages of images:

a downward blur

of watercolour
sunsets,

a swirl
of ink in thin,
paraffin walls,

the windshield
dripping

like raindrops
upon it,

but more
incrementally.

Glass acoustics,
celestial music,

hyaline
instrumentarium:

icy glockenspiel,

  verillons,

windchimes,
armonicas,

glass-harp
watergongs,

bottletrees,

wet mobiles
of mirrors,

and aeolian
tambourines,

a clavicylinder.

Glass resonates
until shattered
by precise song.

Optic anomalies
magnify vision:

meaning, a form

of glassiness,

the misprision

of transparency.

Grain Boundaries

rim   rime

     emery

memory   remora

memoir

     moiré

         mirror

         mirage

image   regime

    gems

edges   emerge

    energy

elegy   elegant

         element

letter   stellar

steel

    steam

         metal

master   sleet

         maelstrom

icestorm   serum

         simulacrum

shimmer   sheer

         meerschaum

echelon   mesh

measure

muse   machinery

from Virtual Realities

VR-1

The condemned prisoner, fed intravenously,
sits locked in an electric chair. The wires
from the chemotrodes implanted in his cranium
lead to a toy trainset on a table beside him.
The miniature locomotive whirs around the track
on the weak current supplied by the electro-
chemistry of his brain. His blank eyes have
rolled back into their sockets from the rictus
of epileptic delirium. The warden calls this
art exhibit *the emancipation of the universe.*

VR-2

The business executive, waiting at the corner
for a taxi, glances down at the curb by his feet
and screams. He does not see the black asphalt
of the road, with its glinting flecks of crystal
grit, but sees instead a precipice that overlooks
an abyss of stars into which he is about to fall.
The paramedic at the scene of the accident later
tells reporters that the mutilated body in the
middle of the street has died from depressurization,
apparently caused by sudden exposure to a vacuum.

VR-3

The assistant technician, staying late after work,
assembles a complex array of lasers and mirrors
in order to generate the perfect hologram of a rose.
He turns off the lights in the studio and fires up
the emitter, the ruby rays interfering with each
other at the centre of the tripods and cameras,
where the spectre of a flower hovers in the dark.
He passes his hand through the image with horror,
unable to tell if he is solid, and the rose
a ghost, or if the rose is solid, and he the ghost.

VR-4

The classical musician, trained in electronics,
knows that soundwaves from ambient noise can leave
their imprint on drying clay. He has insomnia.
He packs a valise with his recording equipment
and uses a borrowed key to break into a museum,
where he puts on his acoustic headphones and runs
a phonographic stylus across a single brushstroke
in the canvas of an impressionist painting.
He hears in the static both a brief shard of music
from a violin and a soft voice saying the word *blue*.

from Silicon Tapestries

---

threadbare carpets
for jacquard looms

byzantine machines

amber cameo persia

pink furrowing
gilt filaments

striae of a screen
video interference

---

ethereal celestina

cobweb of electric
snowstorms

azure cirrus ashes

blueprints of milk
spilt on sapphires

antifreeze
for a flow of data

---

crystalline panels
burgundy nightfall

satin damson glass

embroidered ribbon
nocturne
written in darkest
amethyst

murex ink on paper
mirrors of amnesia

---

electron monorails
floodlit by a star

ice of nothingness

x-ray vacuum photo

obsidian in winter

terraces of silver
as seen from their
thousandth plateau

---

crimson cellophane
for a grand bazaar

white noise trauma

exitsign expressed
in barcode sutures

rubylith labyrinth

traceries of frost
as seen in a fever

---

silicon panopticon

atlas to an insane
asylum for a ghost

fovea nerve cornea

radar surveillance
in rings of a tree

camera of insomnia
robotic eye of god

from Bitstream

000

Information for a machine
forms from any symmetry
in its system of memory
this mystery of rhythms
and rhymes. Any harmony
in the mythic arithmetic
of either theme or meter
is anathema to a theorem
of disorder and discord,
the randomness reminding
us of our odd, modern era.

001

Mass-media has a myriad
dimensions of sensation,
our minds remade to die
on demand for some mad
delirium of melodramas
and dreams. We devise
a device to advise us,
but all that it does is
compute us to come put
us to use in the service
of its servomechanisms.

010

Television, to tell its
visions of invigilance,
envisions us as agents
of an alien intelligence
that tends to enslave us
genetically via virulent
invasion. Vital rivals,
all the trivial viruses
survive us, even in our
victory over the ritual
verity of virtual reality.

101

Imaginary numbers burn
some menagerie of sums
into numb bitstreams
of energy for imagery
in urgent brainstorms,
all because abacuses
xerox zeroes or rezone
ones. Bad data added
to a database debases
the basis for debates
inside our cyberspaces.

Ubu Hubbub
(The Imperial Decree of Ubu Roi)

on behalf of Premier Mike Harris

ubu hubbub
blubbering
rubber gut
a rutabaga
tuba blurb
gluttonous
kettledrum
cumbersome
gummybears
of bourbon

ubu jujube
bungeejump
dungbeetle
jumbo jets
a jamboree
of wombats
jabberwock
lumberjack
jellybeans
of belgium

ubu bamboo
zombie god
bombardier
as bazooka
boom kazoo
gesundheit
ink poodle
nincompoop
no gazebos
go berserk

ubu buddha
ubermensch
troubadour
obese oboe
beelzeboub
boobytraps
scuba gear
juggernaut
of bugaboo
bugger off

from Eunoia

Awkward grammar appals a craftsman. A dada bard damns
stagnant art and scrawls an *alpha*, a small ankh that can
stamp a blatant hallmark and spawn a madcap anagram.
A daft vandal has drawn a slapdash paraph (an arc, slant,
and zag) that warps all stanzas, all ballads: what a prank,
what a scandal. A flaw, a gaff, as flagrant as an aardvark at
a gala ball, mars all paragraphs, all almanacs. A scar, a mark,
that can crack a mandala, warrants a grand drama, a black
psalm. A dark cassandra chants abracadabra as a mantra
and warns that what harms a law can attract bad karma.
A cataclasm starts at dawn as a star falls.

Naphtha gaslamps cast a warm charm. A fat maharajah
basks at a spa, at a bar, that has swank, that has class.
A vassal at hand can grant a pashakhan all palatal manna
that a man can want: jam tarts and armagnac, bran flans
and schnapps. A dwarf, a thrall, can draw a man's bath,
wash a man's back, as spartan lads fawn and hang,
athwart an altar, amaranth garlands as fragrant as attar —
a balm that calms all angst. A shah can catch an act at
a danza, watch pagan gals can-can and cha-cha, catcall
a jazzband that scats a waltz and a samba. A sax drawls
tantaras; maracas rasp cantatas. A lass as sad as a swan
twangs a glass harp.

Brassbands blat jazz razzmatazz. Rapt fans at a bandstand
clap as a fat-cat jazzman and a bad-ass bassman blab gangsta
rap (all a-sharps and a-flats) — a gangland fad that attacks
what Bach and Brahms call art. Gangs and clans that act
as crass as Falstaff clack tankards and harass Harvard grads
at a frat (*gamma kappa lambda*): what a fracas, what a brawl.
Vamps and bawds spank a man's ass and wank a man's
balls. A madam, all schmaltz and sarcasm, dabs at mascara
and nags a barman. A shah, pajama-clad, slaps a call-gal,
snaps a bra-strap, as a dark watchman stands back abaft
an arras and plans a backlash as rampant as wrath.

R. M. VAUGHAN

. . . in sotto howl . . .

3 Poems for Paul Bowles

1. paul and jane

. . . names from children's readers
        or English colouring books
work-a-day   saints' names   hung on the back end of hyphens
           like afterthoughts
names tired mothers give their fifth or seventh child

. . . all grown up and an ocean away, we nap   spines cool
        against whitewash and aqua tile   beds apart
      sexes (punch and judy)   dumbed by 2 pm heat
        we share (only) alike dreams
of Tangiers afternoons under lovers like ourselves (not the other)
of sweating pigments of brown and white and common red
of curing   two skins
        the colour of unleavened bread.

2. *dit moi, m' mohammed*

car   je vu une journée trop long   mais seulement
        un fragment d'un roman, mon roman   tous les même
dit moi
où est la table, la tasse, le kif, les pages?   tous les periodes, grains
inscriptions   pour mon histoire?
                sûr ta peau . . .

m' mohammed   tu as trois femmes et deux hommes
                à le vers entre ton menton et ta aine
                comme la Shiva, comme un ver
m' mohammed   tes livrès sur ma sexe, nôtre peau marron   par nature où
        par choix   dit moi   *je t'aime*   où
quelques chose.

3. the tired place

in the sun, how long I've walked   for stories, a bed
  . . . but rest — it too shuns   still asks to see my papers, calls my hand

some men spit, look away   make noises in the souk
      a slow language
with tongue and water and billowed cheek   (semaphore)
      call me *reguiba blanc*
ask me home

        after mint tea, black cigarettes   always rough mouthing,
        slicked thighs, maybe fists

     . . . everything gets written down, beds are rolled for travel
eyes shut like it or not.

for some of us summer

means we can stop   in the park, sit in trees strung with
fat leaves
— thatch to dull the incessant rain of wedding bells —
            maybe   go down   into bullrushes,
golden
    rod, asters and take up fingersful
of sod and wet blades   'cause
        blank-faced, heads hot from skin-close haircuts
                we're careless;   not watching, not
remembering
to look away, see past   young men's fresh-razored necks,
shirtless arms
                        brown-brown hips   and lower
        our eyes   back down to the one note earth

. . . playing deaf to love songs to college boys, cops, and single
men.

Bed Poem #3

I have done this before —
fingertips flick perfect, identical, plastic buttons,
bottoms up
plumb-level against torso then
                                    slide
each tensed disk, head first, through threaded
almond envelopes;
repeat the trick, count the clasps
one
through
seven:
symmetrical.

I delay unhinging the final piece
de resistance
to tease out his nipples;
to lick the raised moldings of collar bone
and brush, tongue flat, the narrow, hairless plain
between breasts (painting a sloping Y
in saliva);
to dance long figure 8's down the catwalk
from jugular to belt buckle —
the curtains of seam and silk
framing my performance.
We have done this before.

Impatient, the shirt front drifts, curtain call,
over each swollen deltoid, and sinks to pinched waist:
unveiling, full frontal, the curl and rise
of your abdomen and breast
        index fingers trigger
        on my belt loops
        pull me close

release me to the press of biceps
and, at the base of my spine
work lefttorightrighttoleft
to tug and release the fragile breach
of cuff and knotted wrists;
each   with a dangerous   pop

silk strikes the solid line
of glossy woodplanks —
water on oil cloth,
indifferent.

quiet now,
cut nails reach up and over, and down,
testing the tips of shoulder blades,
and dig:
precise, firm, and mindful
of the fragility
of skin.
You have done this before.

Bed Poem #6

In the shallow, pulsing
hollow
between your body
and the sheets   — a grotto,
      tri-cornered, (Isosceles)
      by the smooth
underside
   of your forearm;
         the cleft of your shovel-spade shoulder
               and   (just two finger breadths away)
         your perfect, bark-brown
         eyelet
         nipple —
cover me. Only
make the round
of your bicep
a lid,
and I will fold
in the hollow's font
and rest
curly-cue,
like a crisp Christmas ribbon
stropped on the hull
of a scissor blade:
magnetic.

Bed Poem #8

Actually, this time
everything is done
on a wooden kitchen chair:

me, on bottom, thighs flat under your weight, happy
about connecting
(finally)   square/round peg to round/square hole
lace dry hands under powdered armpits
clasp opposite forearms and bearhug then,
pairing thumbs and indexes
with nipples,
knead milkless teats.

you, husky now with autumn fat
lean into the little pinches, lift up, and, palms flat,
smooth the pink friction between our rubbed-raw legs;
   long fingers
deftly push apart
my inner legs
just enough to share
the rim of the seat

and now,
muscles shifted,
I move up and deep and take
a whole tufted breast
in each hand; so you curl —
fast into my grip, doubleover, pushing against my pull —
and freeze;
your brown spine moored at the base of my sex in a long,
   liquid arch —
we make the beast with two fronts,
a pair of gargoyles in a font
drained for winter, my mouth open
in sotto howl: both of us caught
in the curious silence
of a standoff.

The World of Ice
(after R. M. Ballantyne)

(1)

I know this story — two boys, many men, open spaces, little
    warmth —
I have seen it blue-lit, ashamed of itself,

                                        in cramped quarters:
We have grown bolder   in darker venues
and less alluring
at home   yet, no era is without psychologies
        home truths
someone read this before me and knew

    the up and down slush of ice, of brine, would sugar-coat
        the figurehead   clothing proud breasts, diamond
                                        nipples

. . . a muted siren, her calls, internalized
backfire on us, we turn to each other, only half
from fear

(2)

A Pirate
scarlet, mustachioed, priapic
    his hair tied with kelp, salted grey, cat-black, and olive
waves skull and bones (the Netherworlds)   *Captain Blood*
    a rape fantasy made large
    two womanless ships   collide (engage)

    there is always violence
    in seduction (this is more or less honest)
    so it goes   behind stores of salt pork, hard biscuit, coils
    of scratchy, oiled rope
            and Our Hero buried deep in the stern

gaze; pressed, knees red in the crawl
space —

half-mast on all fours, we wait for the skewer, the plank

(3)

Untimely demise
en scene:
The (present) Father, his chest a barrel
of monkeys —
he is made comic,
        a patron of sex
        tonne-weight, of the wave and ice and whale
for our relief
and release   from responsibility
from love:
good daddy/bad daddy
(it's a mood thing)

today
under the spotlight sun
sleeveless and soiled
his panelled forearms sweat the smell of eucalyptus and mint,
of balms, of healing
leaves — crushed, bottled, and let loose again over sterile froth
and ceaseless ice   envoys from the garden provinces
he has never seen . . .

again, night after night
        (red sky in mourning
as on land, so at sea
        sailors make warming)
— there's one in every port
(and hall)
                hunker down
                        closer, quieter

                    lowslung
          a hundred men in rope beds
                    (The Hanging Gardens)

. . . with each dark the waves
                    will toss
                    and turn our bodies
                    together.

(4)

Fitting of the *Pole*
        — *Star* for the Frozen Seas
sees
a barren caste (off) — men alone, we cannot cast
our (frozen) seed   anymore — but, underneath our hull
  skin, tar-pitched
Desire
still runs, cuffs the under-ice, hides in pockets, chides
(almost) silently.

Black-fevered, Desire   mars our woolen quilts,
                        (patched in spring, after shearing virgin rams)
        twists our straw wheat pallets
      (stuffed mid-summer, by womens' unsuspecting hands)
        makes us forget the life of Seasons
        of May poles, swarming harvest rites, women
        and men.

        Desire
. rebukes the flawless
cobalt-white glare of transformed water
and crystallized salt . . .

(good) Daddy
his chest   mossy, warm
the only thing alive
out here:
when I travel, what I despise
at home
I come to love.

(5)

The water is a flat, moving mirror
stretching my face fun-house long
        . . . on deck, we keep our chins, all eyes, close to the fore
        most task, minding the aft —
                                terse thoughts, tongue, glances
clear the deck
cadences of whitecaps keep
our heads to our work
all hands   to ourselves

at night, at appointed times, between shifts
        and long pants and flannels
small eyelets of cotton open   (loop-holes

to muscle   in our cont(r)act)
and vein and hair — a game   for fingers
like splicing or
        cat's cradle: hands cold, pale from Northern
                passages found, find
                a split
                in the ice   white linens
                then   warmed
                close again, never record
                                (oral history)
        The Transgression.

from Sickness Lexicon

(3) guilt

in bed
we play it cool
and inessential:
my body,
adorned,
like an amber-coffined
beatle;
treasured,
like a granite-brilliant
fossil fish — an artifact
contained.
Your eyes,
dull as peeled thumbnail
husks, their lashes
curling, sickle-fine, abject,
refocus:
Tonight we'll play cause
and affect, though
my tongue,
my frothing lip-corners,
are cum-dry
from charities
overstepped, overbitten,
(solutions) over-chewed.

There was a dry sense of promise the morning
I arrived, unshaven;
a citric taste of work-to-be-done. But
    In a dream,
    later,
    I was with you, and
    we were stealing things, left and
    right, in a crayon store decorated in leaping,

scissor-peaked, blue/orange cartoon flames
— a bonfire staged to look
like hell — and
you flourished a gunsize,
white Crayola. So
we scribbled
over the flames,
breaking their uniform triangles,
denying their crisp
certainty,
and ran
for our lives.

(8) nature/nurture

As if food
were dirt,
I cleaned my plate;
Because I was a vacuum,
(abhorred by nature)
I ate my fill:
saturation, dependency,
and re-
saturation. This Appetite,
grown exponentially,
like a chain link perimeter
see-through yet
hermetic,
shaped   so much
of my compliance,
my grammar,
the   doing-what-I-was-told,
that I felt safe
against the net.

Because I remembered
nothing but
All or Nothing But,
I played it
where I'd laid.
(Every man
for himself
is a double entendre
where I come from.)

So
how can you come to me now,
— me, lately such
slim pickins' —
with empty collection plates

of Poverty
Abstinence
and Obedience —
a (silenced) groaning board,
steaming in your latex claws
and expect anything
but spit
and kicking feet?
You, who know how well
I've been trained
to crack open each shell and
get at its meat.

Half empty/half full is acculturation
gone mad.
(Featureless,
I stuffed my face
to remove the very question;
full-
fillment
became my second
second nature.)

Now you'll teach us
to blame the habitué, not the habits;
to spare our rods
lest we spoil your children.
Now, (so soon, considering)
my mouth must not water
at the ringing chimes
— I am excused
from the experiment —
no,
now, I am only to hear
gentle music,
not signals;

to appreciate intangible
orchestrations
without meaning.

At best,
this is the sound of an alarm;
not the dinner bell,
not the clanging promise
of sustenance —
    this is music
to mourn by.

M*A*S*H Notes for Private Kyle Brown

things I know about you, Private Kyle Brown

you are in jail. a teenage boy from a country most of our people
can't find on a map (me included) is dead. you are involved. you
have forearms like wide hard hammers. you work out in prison,
twice a day. you have tits as full as autumn pears,
nipples meeting abs in a hard, fatty line and that's fine. you are a
right wing media star.

pardon me, I have a bias for soldiers

things I think about you, Private Kyle Brown

you are a liar and a coward. you were in love with Corporal
Clayton Matchee and now that he's basically dead to the world
you're thinking my heart is broken so I want what's mine.
Corporal Clayton Matchee was taller than you and the desert is
cold at night (I understand).
      you did nothing, you did nothing, with a room full of
guns, a foreign permissive sky, all the right ideas on your side
you did nothing.
you are a liar and a coward.
      I hate you because you did nothing.

forgive me, I have a problem with team players

around the same time Private Kyle Brown decided to keep his
love alive and not Shidane Arone   it was dark in Toronto
and early in the day and 3 boys, forearms hard and wide as
hammers, stood around my village, my part of town,
my home   3 boys waited for me, kicked me, spat on me

3 boys said queer queer queer fucking queer   in a way not
embracing the concept of reclamation and one boy (with the ugli-
est face and therefore the most to prove) said I've got a gun your
face I'm gonna blow off

around the same time Private Kyle Brown decided the chance of a
drunken bear hug after the kill beat Shidane Arone's chance for a
decent life   I was not as afraid as I should have been because 2
leather fags tall as cops, forearms hard and wide as planks,
walked past and I waited to be rescued

nothing   they did nothing

with a street full of fags and gym earned muscles and all the
new gay power on their side they decided to keep their love literally
alive and not (maybe) me
        only the traffic, a spring coat satisfyingly covered in spit,
plus teenage boredom intervened

I hope you'll understand I have a bias against bystanders

things I feel these coincidences in our lives should tell you, Private
    Kyle Brown
don't you ever say "scapegoat"
never, never ask for that   you are a coward and a liar and I have
    seen my share
don't you ever say "cover up"
when your face is everywhere

was it really so simple as the safety of the word nigger?

things I cannot say to you in person, Private Kyle Brown
because you are in prison

I don't believe you.   because Corporal Clayton Matchee
was tall and his forearms met his elbows like the bent axle from
the Jeep that blew up in the sand 4 days before you landed   love
or a teenage boy   from a country most of our people cannot find
on a map of the world (including me)   wasn't
really a choice, was it?

I'm glad you are in prison because cowards frighten me.
loving murderers is easy it's maintaining the relationship that kills.
your forearms are like hammers, flat and hard.
you will never make colonel.   and it was love, or Shidane
    Arone   but
somehow the two became one   and you could share his death
    with Corporal
Clayton Matchee   and maybe that was consummation

in the videotape on TV you look down a lot and I do that too —
a perverse reaction to tall men, to see their feet — looking up is
savouring   but I noticed you looked straight down into the
camera for the cover of *Saturday Night* maybe you saw
upside down in the lens   what Shidane Arone saw from the pit
you killed him in   the pathology of infatuation, of a face
starry-eyed, happy at last to share a secret with a lover, a secret
more powerful than latrine misdemeanors or shower tent suckoffs
a secret for a lifetime
maybe you saw the future, your face, always and forever after
out of context you saw   The Murderer's Lover, the smallest
character in the third act
of any opera I know

remember, you get one song, one costume change, one death
(off stage)

(coda)
things I know about opera that could help you understand your life
from now on, Private Kyle Brown

the part of the Murderer's Lover is often cut for budgetary
reasons or, even more devastating, dramaturgy.
the Murderer's Lover is traditionally represented by simple
costume, a painted teardrop.
the Murderer's Lover must be able to double for comedic parts
such as the Innkeeper, or a Blind Man.
the Murderer's Lover is a boy, a boy, a boy.

the name of the Murderer's Lover is forgotten by the audience
in the lobby   (Antonia? Almodevera?)
the actor who played the Murderer's Lover is forgotten
   by the critics
at the coat check   (American, isn't he?)
the one solo allowed the Murderer's Lover is forgotten by the
   other actors
during the first cigarette break   (hum it for me again?)

the face of the Murderer's Lover, covered in blood, never
   registers on stage.

At Arm's End

rests the small red and black radio
brought to me one Pride Day
      because I never read the papers
at arm's end, between restless fingers
I twist a pleat of ice-blue pillowcase
turned navy by your sweat
and mine;
at arm's end (just)
behind your lucky, sleeping head
an excited voice, ignorant of the remembrance that carries it
  — a token
of Stonewall parades and last Sundays in June (kept)
before and after my own —
breathes a booming sigh of relief,
tells me to sleep a little easier; tells me we are at an end to arms
and all Threats are removed — wars are again   remote
soldiers   worn out
               I stretch
                  over you — my
                      forearm grazing your half-inch hair
                  and stop the voices
                  blustery with Peace
                  and Security never offered me
                  and mine.

currents and particles spit testily until
the dull click of the plastic dial at my arm's   end stirs you and
half-awake   tonight like the rest of the world   (but not
at rest while so unlike)
you push air through shut teeth and answer
"hold me
nothing was won in our name."

KEVIN CONNOLLY

I've misread the directions again . . .

They Remain Hatless

"Marooned" was the wrong word for it.
Say, instead, "stuck" with "this shallow panic."
Not articulate but . . . that other thing,
the bald thoughts remain hatless in a

flash flood of monogrammed confetti.
"All Hail," a bored crow offers,
the end, it seems, is close at hand again.
You wear those shallow cuts as

an itinerary of minor renovations, all
your hard thought turned pale and
vanished with the cordless sun.
What's left now is only dark-*ish*

really, not nearly so wild or
impressive as I had hoped.

Raw Dough
for Arthur Penn

He used to think that if he
looked the bullets in the eye
they'd freeze somehow — like
rodents on a wild highway —
find their own weight and tumble
to the pavement. He sees now
he'd been wrong about all that,
hot metal imploding the car doors,
hammering out the glass in
a few satisfying thuds.
The flight bag on the seat beside
him isn't living up to its name
just now. Inside, bundles of cold
cash in lottery sequence.
From under the dash he tries the dead
engine again while metal wasps fall
through the chassis in horizontal downpour,
all tooth and thick-headed weight.
He rolls over her wet slump,
feeling a handful thrown through
him into her. Before the day goes out
completely he wills the door open
(or is that also the bullets?)
tugging at her feebly as he moves.
The last hope of live escape is
trickling red feathers on the vinyl,
and so he will picture it instead —
an alternative stylish closing:
accidental gunman cutting down
some brilliant evasion, a single
bullet travelling through both hearts,
an end wilder than their wild lives.
The red curtain dropped over rising eyes;
the forest of slender onlookers,
spinning to a stop.

Junkmale

I wonder if we'd all calm down
a little if sex were a seasonal thing,
like fruit ripening. If all you
had to do was sit in the wet dirt
and wait for the carrot to scream.

In my dream, Madonna
is shitty in bed. She's
hard and kind of boney and
bellows "Respect Yourself!"
the whole time.

There's a tired-looking waitress
at the bar at the end of the street
who wears shiny low-cut blouses.
She's circled the bar with typewriters,
one typewriter for each gaunt regular.
"One day," she tells me, "One of
these MEN is going to write me
into a novel."

I've just spent the whole fucking night
playing pool with Bob on a threadbare,
half-size, buck-a-play table.

"Research," I call it.
Bob calls it "Thursday,"
and he's right.

Arbitrary Cultures

What do you think is
meant by "a healthy dose?"
Sour clouds are spilling
against the metal hills
like stained bees
spinning to a stop
against a window screen.

I'm sure you'll be impressed
when I tell you the vines
have split, gnawed themselves
off at the root and blown away.

The lights go on at Wrigley Field;
a world resigns itself to shallow desperation.
Phonographs are shouting dance
dance dance dance dance-to-the-radio,
and I guess there's sense in that.
The lilies tremble under the aquaducts,
night sharpens its knuckles on the hot asphalt.

We will make the best of these mistakes:
settle on the secret ingredients,
rearrange the rubbled cities
into quaint cliffside towns.

We will put our shoulders
to the grim bluff of science,
repopulate ourselves
one street at a time.

Progress Report

The way the rain runs up the street
afraid of drowning,
the spitting roof tipped below the
window as I take my seat.
Today, my legs are broccoli-coloured.
I have webbed feet.
Pinned open on the kidney tray
I wait for a nervous student
to misidentify my pancreas.

The rain gusts and turns the windows
into Woolworth's soda fountains.
Trees jump back from a moving street
like startled chickens;
the leaves quiver,
silver arrows pointing
at a stunned sky.

I have a memory like this:
out the back of the house
as a child, watching the storm
roll over the field, hanging
on the silo of the vacant farm,

the odd bird shouting at the grass,
and gusts of wind actually
blowing through my head,
leaving it sharp
and crisp as an apple.

My life, at worst, has been conducted in
a light drizzle. Though I have seen two
plane crashes . . . one only tall flames
at the village airport, the other
a Blue Angel at the Ex —
his wing dipped a teaspoon from the lake
and he was gone in a cough of flame.

When he was in the airforce
Dad bailed out over Quebec,
but he was back in three days
with only a frightened wife
and insect bites to contend with.

Nothing very dramatic has happened since —
a couple of car accidents, couple
of people I didn't know much dying.
School. Two pennant races,
a few shit jobs.

Even the rain's not very dramatic.
It couldn't put out the
fire on that pilot's airsuit.
It can't even get through
a thin wall of glass.

Still, it pushes you inside
and breathes on you,
messing up the order of a few years,
forcing a little long grass
up through the bald lawns of
what is now suburbia.

It hangs over the drawer
of my short life putting
wrong things together:
a hammer and two screws,
a ball of string and an
unmailed letter,
an eraser and a matchbook —

small, useful things I keep,
but have no home for.

Order Picker

Category Four: Horsemanship

I lose a broken watch,
then dream I am my father.

Category Twelve: Fidelity

The python licks
the cold mirror.

Category Seventeen: Faith

A group of flightless birds
admired by thieves.

Category Eighty: An Anecdote

I invent a strange instrument,
motorless and unassembled.

Category Seventy-Six: Advancement

The black hill; a heavy cloud
grasps its own unfolding.

Angel Food Cake

My desperation showers in
its own loveliness, presets the oven
at 350 degrees, and prepares
a lemon basting sauce.

I've misread the directions again.

I decide Love is a slow meandering from pain
and my dyslexic knots outdo themselves
hissing *yes yes yes*
among the columns.

The moon plays peekaboo
with the clouds like a
starlet pulling the sheets
up over her breasts
after the love scenes,

scenes which feature
windows and crumpled clothes
on a chair, the quivering leaves
shadowed on the wall, but never,
never the wet flesh of the actors.

Adolf Earns His Iron Cross

I thought we had already decided
on packing it in, but the corporal,
understandably, wasn't let in
on the conference, though I don't
think anyone expected this
kind of trouble from him.

He's rattling on in his little voice
over his black waxed moustache,
some nonsense about Madame Blavatsky
and the psychic history of the great races,
a destiny which, no doubt, includes some
missing limbs or large holes
in the chest for many of us
before it's over.

I'm looking at Gustav's tin cup,
half-filled with mud,
and the crack in the toe of my boot
which sucks water like a wound
when I move my toes.

I've stopped listening,
but I can see it in
the grey faces of the others.
They've straightened up,
and their feet have stopped shuffling.

One of the privates brushes
a clot of mud from his overcoat.

"Stop Pulling My Hair,"

Betty says, slapping the lobster on his nasty, boiled claw.
Meanwhile, in the barbecue pit, an outraged Paul and Linda
have snatched the bleeding patties from the grill, and are
giving them a decent burial in the shrubbery.

On the patio, the professors are weeping with disappointment,
sent home by the administration to await reassignment.

Right here, beside my ear, the windows swarm and buzz
against the traffic, and suddenly I know that in a thousand
living rooms across this great city, the favourite child is
squatting, ready to plant a fork in the electric socket.

Number Seventeen

I

The newspapers reported that some time that night
a gust of cold breath disturbed
some dry leaves in a wooded glen.
"A soundless gasp, that's all,"
said the minister responsible,
"like steam escaping from a long-cold train."

II

The next night, the minister receives
a phone call from his Times contact.
"Go to the river," he rasps into the phone
beside his sleeping wife,
"take the blade between your fingers and whistle.
take the reed between your teeth and
breathe from underneath.
Wait for me to come."

III

The water is dark and biting,
the reporter's fingers are too cold to whistle
to the minister, climbing into the shadows
on the riverbank. Slowly, he numbs,
then slips like paper into the current.
The bridge soars over the river like a slide-rule.
The night collapses. Black glass.

IV

"Where is it?" someone shouts.
Underneath the floorboards, down the hall.
"Where is she?" asks the minister.
She's the derailment in number seventeen.

V

Number seventeen did not like her meal.
Number seventeen has landed a soap commercial.
Number seventeen is not the face of the murdered girl.
Number seventeen would be advised to test the market.
Number seventeen is not without friends in high places.

VI

Beads of sweat on the minister's brow.
Number seventeen spits at him, claws
at his socks, shakes him feverish from sleep.
Underneath the clogged sink are the same tools,
the same unopened detergents.

Each morning is a new challenge.
He notices everything, the expressions
of the men and women as they pass him in the street,
beneath each shallow face the clear, lingering
scent of bloody laundry.

VII

And still he looks for her,
in the streets and the convenience stores,
in phosphorescent malls filled with
astronauts and beehive hairdos,
plucked lips and self-adhesive
bathroom tiles.

VIII

Number seventeen includes these matching endtables.
Number seventeen is a long way from home.
Number seventeen has a wearying caseload.
Number seventeen is the winning caller.
Number seventeen went a lot smoother
than one through sixteen.

IX

Number seventeen stares up awkwardly from
the bed, split skull screaming accusations,
spilling liquid like a cafeteria in heat.
Number seventeen is bundling up the limbs
into neat metallic packages it's
reeling off one-liners
and stumbling over doorjambs it's
out in the street screaming "Search Me!"
at the top of its lungs it's
coughing up blue suits it's
burying the minister
in cold, white kisses.

Face

It's the perfect cocktail party;
his own voice, pronouncing for the others.

Philosophy is nothing more
than God throwing his voice.
The face is the mind's puppet,
and tell me, who of us can
drink and speak at the same time?

Trapped in booths, guests
supply the required questions.
One hand dispenses praise, the other
punishes those whose faces
brighten before the answer is given.

In the dream, his real complexion
is obscured by trivia: eyes, nose,
a mouthful of crumbling teeth.
Sometimes it ends here,
and sometimes there's a yearning

to get underneath, to
penetrate a softer surface.
To loosen the material
at the fingertips and bring
the contours to attention;

to bend the neck back, and leave
in each ear a dull persuasion:
the feeling that it all
might change,

that things aren't nearly
as ornate as they pretend to be.

"Symbols are Lice,"

he said, or "cymbals are lies,"
but the connection was breaking
up and it was a wrong number anyway.
I was stringing him along with
noncommittal answers,
pretending, when he said
"Al, my marriage is falling apart,"
that I'd heard my name instead.
If he found me out later,
I would say he sounded exactly
like a friend on the phone,
or a friend in a snowstorm of static,
or a little like a friend I knew
a long time ago, before puberty
even, and this was how I imagined
his voice would change and how
he would confide in me about his
marriage if he in fact was married by now.

The line was breaking up,
we had what they call
a bad connection, and it occurred
to me that this could be
one of those times you
sort of tuned in
to someone else's conversation,
and then it bothered me to think
of even my neutral, insincere answers
slipping into nowhere,
while (of course) I missed
the comforting part, the part where
Al was reassuring Len or Dave, or whatever
stranger's name resembles most closely

a friend who I could recall quickly,
and maybe rattle off a few details about
to avoid the suggestion that this was
mere voyeurism on my part, or
whatever it is when you
intentionally listen in on
someone's private conversation
because you want to know, you
need to know what Al
might have to say about love and betrayal
and the outmoded nature of monogamy
in these our changing times.

But of course that would be
the part you can't hear,
while what you can hear
is straight and boring and familiar,
the kind of muffled pain
an aspirin might take care of,
if an aspirin could answer the phone
and be there for a friend,
be there to say take me,
take me twice,
and call Al in the morning.

Hurtin' Song

"Woah, brother, she
done lef' me high an' dry
as kindling,"
a wet bug drifting
in a patio ashtray after
a loathesome winter rain.
The terrain is familiar, dear,
all wail and warts
and stale sorrows resurrected by
the buzzing car stereo.

Does she hate me?
Are her eyes ships, slipping
port and starboard in
my souvenir ballpoint?
Does the breeze part her hair
like a dutchman's arrow, thudding
to a stop in thin air?

My eyes are tiring and the
night reveals none of the
dour secrets she hides away
like carrots from the longtooths.
My heart's stuffing stripped
from its rusty spring
while it rains guitar picks
all over Sticky Street.

"Uncle"

I call you my "symptom,"
my "afternoon peach;"
I'm your "punch-drunk semaphore,"
guiding in the under-rotated 'copters.
Ah, I remember it well,
glinting like a poor-broke penny
in your bald-floored corral,

last straw used   (sucking back a Coke),
sawdust squandered   (a wet arson's nightmare).

Together we'll stalk the flaccid hour
with a TV news crew; confused,
clinging to the wind bent hill,
settling on something "settled."

In the meantime, we're all free agents,
gov-docs in designer underclothes,
tapping at the pet shop glass
with pencils and hangnails and quarters,
contrary to the explicit instructions
of the proprietors.

We've slipped ham sandwiches
into the condom dispensers,
trussed the emergency exits
with firehose. Hot dog vendors
draft terms on napkins
in squeezable yellow mustard.

At sundown, the management surrenders.
There'll be ample time to argue
the rudiments of safe egress,
the relative sentience of the domestic pig.

We'll argue till the cows come home,
dragging their fart-produced ozone holes
like an October tailwind
hauls a Goodyear Blimp —
the "Step Smartly" of Akron, Ohio.

Today I'm seeing gravesites
in the Dumpsters, my name
and health card number
hidden carefully, a prize
under the rim of a paper cup.

All crimes are becoming one crime,
these slivers of confluence
just hearsay evidence.
See now, how that one preens,
how this one is erased by doubt.
Sad, blue, sequestered road of cures:
those little empty spaces
no one's thought to walk.

ESTA SPALDING

What falls from us finds no place . . .

Eggs

My mother cracks eggs
into the cast iron skillet.
Taps them on the edge
then thrusting thumb into crack
pulls out their jelly insides.
How do you want them?
We are on stools, toes pointed
at the cracks between linoleum slabs.
We won't step on those.
Scrambled, poached?
Kristin spins through air
like a whisk in milk
          outside the low belch of septic tank
she says, *I'll never brush my hair again.*
It hangs a pale web around her neck.
Where do eggs come from?

When she was born
I painted my body black,
waited on the steps for the car to come home,
when she emerged pink and glazed
I clutched her to blackness,
anointed, immaculate.
Marks on my body where hers had been.

From birds, my mother says.
I wait, like I waited for the pork chop
to cook in my Betty Crocker oven
came back days later to find a plate
of maggots I had made from meat.
Their bodies, tiny fingers
the colour of cream. I grew
them in my oven: a whole

box of maggots
that ate until they grew wings.

We are in the kitchen spinning,
legs wide open.

I can raise the dead.

Backyard Growing Up

She planted the *be still tree*
over the septic tank. It grew red,
vibrant with waste's luxury. Every Saturday
it was trimmed, the whole lawn raked,
in a ceremony of what's commonplace.

Twice a week we ate fast-food specials: hotdogs,
fries, root beer, one dollar. We spun
in the plastic chairs, our tanned colt's legs
hanging over the edge, our arms thrust out
like blades, we sang: *I walked one morning*
by the sea and all the waves reached out to me.
My mother made us share our fries.

Sometimes we only bought seventy-two cents
worth of gas. Sometimes we had bad dreams.

We sang loud and wanted nothing.
When I was twelve she bought me a rose bush.
Every week a new bud appeared, a jewel
made from dirt.

Was I the weeds we learned to name
in school: *welfare rose, showy tick,*
bastard poppy, loosestrife?

My mother combing my hair
as I ran for the bus to school
or making leis on May Day
with blossoms from the backyard.

At night, my sister and I prayed
to the Cricketman
asking for the chance to sing,
for louder voices,
the *be still tree* below our window.

Salt
for Sark

thrown past the dash
board   in neutral   no gas
six-pack between your legs
we bumped   dropped
free fall
down Wilhelmina Rise
in a four-wheel-drive
ford   the Pacific below

do you still drive like you surf
an artist of thrill and slice
suturing skin of tube, asphalt gut?

after all these years, it's your heart
that pulls me over the hills

if i could dry you
like sea on rocks,
i'd carry you with me: a salt rodeo,
bucking horses   trucks
striking road and rise

Bread

Who says the body's only 2/3 water?
What myth was told to us?
In the swimming pool with all of you
there was no separation of solid and liquid.
We sublimated, moving between
your skin and mine, your mucus and mine.
Our heavier parts shed themselves,
a chemical reaction, the temperature rising.
On the horizontal together.
Where else do bodies meet on this plane?

My shoulders ached at the end of a day: the ball
and socket having ground, oh, the flour
we milled, the butter churned,
a whole city lit by the motion of arching arms,
by the snap of tendons, and the beating
of all those hearts, a factory of hearts!

The swimmer is pure and Godly number,
the mathematics of pull and torque,
pace, angle, breath, lap, turns,
the time between intervals and sets.
(The bubbles that shouldn't have been on my fingertips,
I carried too much air in my hands!) And the meter:
there was the record I broke in the quad cities
swimming my 500 in 3/4 time
to the rhythms of Muddy Waters,
angry and blue, and me a Chicago Girl —
what music was in this labor!

I toast you
Kris Novak who dove into Wenniger's puke,
finishing the race anyway,

and Tord Alshabkhoun who said
Rotate your torso. Read the backstroke flag.
And Coach Fober, for throwing kickboards
when I thought my legs were through,
and for the eternal fishtail
in a crummy van
on slick Midwestern roads.
You drove us from one corn town to the next.

Thanks, because my body
isn't a border, and water isn't the baptism,
that was a myth too; it's the holy meal,
bread of a thousand.

Then

for Jonathan Green

Then there was the night in the Burgundy Valley
we drove the Quatre-L in the rain.
Wiper blades clearing a blurred V, shoulder
blades hunched over the steering wheel.

Thatched roofs, dirt street
fourteenth-century madonnas
miraculous, bleeding rain.

Where sunflowers grew,
a man in black tie, refusing a ride,
led us through the village to the *grillée*.
A cow, a child watched.

I will forget prayers,
dogs I have sung to,
the maiden name of my grandmother,
but never the angle of your elbow tipped
in rain.

And you were singing Bob Dylan then,
and even then,
I ached for the girl, and the cow,
and the tuxedoed man shrouded in a towel,
and even then for you.

Snapshot

What made me mad was the picture.
The snapshot I had of you
in my kitchen, cutting onions
for a pot of ragout.
It was a good dinner — you with that grinning
face, making love to the camera
and everyone else.

But it's the snapshot that made me mad.
That I had it in my head,
that face of yours halfway
around the world. On the airplane, it fell
between my pillow
and the ashtray. On the beach,
it lay in the sand.
The stupid sand that came back
with me too, in the cracks of my skin
in the gapes of my shoes.

Halfway around the globe
and I had to shake the sand from your
hand on the knife.

What the Cookbook Doesn't Say

Soak the dogfish in lemon juice to neutralize —
One half teaspoon for each pound of meat
                    — The Dogfish Cookbook

The night after the slaughter, I was underwater,
I could breathe.
Drenched with salt,
I waited for your brief
touch across the sheets,
your hand in the bucket of the bed.

I had watched you on the stones
beside the sea, press the heads of dogfish
onto nails driven into carving boards.

Up to your elbows in blood,
the filleting knife
gripped in your webbed fingers,
with the other hand
you pulled the living pups
from their mother's gut,
releasing them into the bucket.
At once, butcher, midwife.

My desire explained
in the baked heat of the rocks,
between the bodies of dogfish:
I am torn
born in your hands.

Moving In

We begin to have the same dreams.
Yours are of fish, huge silent herds
moving through dark waters.

This is because you are returning
to school. You will study fish,
the lateral lines,
how the slightest touch
can move the direction of the whole,
how they lead each other from what
would devour them, how
they seem to be one fish.

I accept this — my head on the pillow
touching yours. Your dreams leap upstream.
I can hardly dream without the flash
of scales in reflected light, the dapple
of us moving side by side.

In the past, I dreamt of a hook
or of little fish in the belly
of big fish in the belly
of biggest.

But I like this: one body
made from many
moving together.

Fall

On these nights that fall early
when leaves drop, mottled,
like the wings of insects who die
in the name of summer,
on these days when flames lick
the iron teeth of grates,
when women swathe themselves in dark cloth
and begin to save eggs, when everything is preserved
against the possibility of decay,
I crawl inside the tenuous nest of sleep.

Things grow uncertain. Plots change.
You have said you will always love me,
but your back is out, your face is framed
with the look of the one who got away.
We have spent hours together tying
the tomatoes to wooden stakes
with a twine so frail it cannot promise
anything. We watch the same movies
over and over
knowing all endings are subject to change,
in the way that leaves will drain
their chlorophyll revealing red.

The characters turn
mean, a woman's murderer
may be her fiancé, may be
the detective, the clock hands
change place,
and we are falling back onto a new hour
that darkens early.
Your attention strays.
All my clothing grows sleeves and legs.

I am bound to my neck in wool
when I step outside to recover
the few in leaves, in nests
made of twigs and string
who wait for a body to deliver them
from the fall.

Getting Back

Take the long way round
the island to that cove pocketed
between hill and sea. Lanikai.
One path into, one path out of — they rise
to the Point that hangs over reef.
                                    Pull over
beside the Chevy junkers, old Mustangs,
dangling dice from their mirrors, brilliant
feathers, hash pipes.
When you were 10 you were afraid
of these men, their engines
back fired, drag-racing past your window
each night — in daylight
you watched through tinted glass
as they slid needles in or tipped
bottles back, the butt
of an oily gun between the thighs.
Each one of them a spark and you, innocent
dynamite.
            Now you meet their glazed eyes.

Tilt your head back to see perched
above rocks the Bird Woman's house,
she lives alone, sleeps on a bed
carved from volcanic cliff.
                            Kick up
your kick stand, pedal the last few rounds.
Coast down into Lanikai.

The air shifts: salt so heavy you taste it.
Tiny yards filled with coconut trees, stubble of itchy
grass, and dried coconuts cracked
by tiny trees that stab up
from dark insides.

Pass Rose and Mary's place
where the tire hangs from a rope
slung over the banyan tree, its roots above
ground and taller than telephone poles. Pass Alani's
where you spent the afternoon
on the porch, in the castaway cardboard box
that brought her mother's new fridge.
Alani, Keithi Jones, and you taking turns
taking off your shorts. Nobody knew, but
you emerged wise. All three of you vowed
to jump on Alani's bed 1,000 times, and you did it too.
You had never believed 1,000 was a number
to be counted to. You flew up on 999,
like three stray planets, came down and then went
up again. Somewhere between 999 and 1,000
you decided life wasn't going to scare you.

Keep pedalling, if your old legs are tired, stand
on the pedals one at a time, it takes 105
to roll you home. It's just as you expected: two stories
tall — the highest house in the neighbourhood.
The roof still droops down, the steps
to the second floor are on the outside, the old red van
is pulled up in the drive. Mynah birds bitch
in the hibiscus, their bright yellow eyes
target you. You have arrived.
You will step back inside, hear
the clatter of Rob, the silversmith who lived
downstairs, who melted a bracelet
around your arm when you turned 10
and gave you a toke from his pipe.
(15 years ago, someone shot him in the head).
You'll take the stairs 2 at a time, and inside

all those fish you overfed, their silver bellies
rising to the surface, will be alive.
Your mother will be soaking soy beans and listening

to the Beatles. The kettle singing to the glass
window slates, dusty in afternoon sun.
Throw down your bike. But before
you go in: close your eyes, count
as high as you can.

When the Box Arrived

Express mail from Honolulu (all
those vowels in the postman's mouth
were white puffs in cold air). I ran upstairs
dug for scissors to cut through string, packing
tape, slid off the lid that said *handle with care*, tenderness
à la Canada Post. Below the tissue
paper:
        strands and strands
of ginger blossoms, delicate as the thread that held
them. The equator's fragile snow.
A box transporting
the reflection of moon in water, the moment
when branches bend, the sky
between azure and storm. That scent
like raining honey
filled the room,
Pacific air in every musty corner —
four of us ankle-deep in mud
tromped upstream beside the river's skirt. Mosquitoes
big as guavas sang
in our ears, blood and insect guts under our nails,
water pooled in palm frond saucers, our eyes
drunk on colour: hibiscus, bougainvillea, bird
of paradise. Up river, carrying Japanese shears
to snip ginger that would wither
before we reached home.

Journey

All day long the pieces
the pieces
falling   saying
how to make sense
     the hawk by road side, face deep
     in the strings of a dog's belly, two deer running beside four
     lanes of highway, necks taut as straining ropes, panic cata-
         pulting them forward, shocked eyes,
              murderous hooves.
The rest stop
     a dead man upright
in the cabin of his truck
beside him
his wife's mouth moves, she is saying
bits of things
     he was just here
     he just slumped
her red lips
hands curled, the tips of her
fingers twitching, holding her coat, she
is saying *We were going to Florida*
     We have friends in Florida
eyes pitched wildly.

What falls from us finds
no place,
         nothing to hold.

Politics

Tanks rolled into Tiananmen Square, as you leaned over to me, across the formica table of *Le Bar Sportif*. How grass-green your eyes were — I had just learned your name, also Green, I was laughing, on the screen soldiers croaked through loud-speakers at students assembled there.

We talked politics. I couldn't look away from you — long brown throat tipped back, slender glass in your left hand, deep brown liquid, like a woman's blood, sliding into your mouth. I wanted to. So angry about those men your lips, eyes brightened as you spoke of them. On my napkin you wrote André Malraux, *La Condition Humaine*.

These were my politics: you across the table, a bend in your elbow, a dimple at the wrist as if you had been kissed (who was it?), your long fingers on the pen, curl of each letter like soft hairs between the legs — over my head, supple bodies before the tanks.

River

It requires precision to move
over you, excavating
your geography, river beds,
gulleys, plates that shift
leaving fragments extruded —
fossil, petrified
shell, a chipped stone adze
as when I touched your tailbone
and you remembered in a fleeting (shadow
of a dream) your first dead.
The girl in your fifth grade class
dead in an accident, car whirling into
the ravine — a fall day, wet crimson leaves melted
to curved road — that time of year, the word *fall*
came to mean
skidding over the edges of things, this
vocabulary forgotten until
I touched you and you recalled praying,
praying for her on your knees, as if each joint
in your body were a rosary bead to be smoothed
for her passing, as if you were the one chosen
to forge her path glistening into heaven
you took her into your
body, slick leaves, hard cells
of black concrete, swallowed with the swollen prayer,
river prayer, the road over the edge was
a river she stepped into — you would follow
her, pack your own vivid body into the absence
behind the car, and slip
into her river, slip her death
into you,
something solid, lodged compactly
at the base of the spine

an artifact any careful lover
might dust with her brushes
and seeing its amber, its red, discern
the burnished coin
to weight the eye of the dead.

Compasses

The jellies haven't forgotten
everything, though they no longer sting
(tentacles shrivelled for centuries).
They grow in a salt lake, remnant itself
of oceans that receded
as pain dulling after a wound.

What the jellies remember is the sun.
Brainless skin pods, they rise
each morning, move in swarms
(transparent bees, a cloud

                          of clouds)
six miles every morning
parting the lake's element, a pulse
travelling a nerve, they careen
towards the sun.
Compasses in full bloom.

Floating gardens,
                     creatures who harbour
plant cells under thin membranes.
Fragile as Japanese lanterns,
lit with chlorophyll, they are farmers
eating what they tend,
migrating each morning, sinking
at night to the lake's darkest layer
to fertilize.
What they are
is what has not quite been
forgotten, memory
insisting itself
a dull globe dipping
into dark and sometimes rising.
A luminous garden
               sails to light.

CONTRIBUTORS

Christian Bök was born in Toronto in 1966. His first collection, *Crystallography* (Coach House Press, 1994), was shortlisted for the Gerald Lampert Award for best poetry debut in Canada, and is the first book in a projected trilogy called *Information Theory*. Bök has received critical acclaim not only for performing Kurt Schwitters' *Ur Sonata*, a soundpoem written in gibberish, but also for producing *Bibliomechanics*, a textmachine built out of Rubik's Cubes.

Kevin Connolly, born in 1962 in Biloxi, Mississippi, is a Toronto-based poet, critic, and short story writer. He is the author of *Asphalt Cigar* (Coach House Press, 1995), and numerous small press chapbooks, including *Losers* (Streetcar Editions, 1991), *Deathcake* (Proper Tales, 1991), and *The Monika Schnarre Story, as told to . . .* (Pink Dog, 1993). As a critic, his work has appeared in such places as *The Brick Reader, Books in Canada, The MacMillan Anthology, West Coast Line*, the *Toronto Star, This Magazine*, and the *Vancouver Review*. Connolly was co-founder and co-editor (with Jason Sherman) of the influential literary magazine *WHAT!* from 1985–1994. He now serves as arts editor for *This Magazine*.

Laura Lush was born in Brantford, Ontario, in 1959. Her first book of poetry, *Hometown*, was published by Véhicule Press in 1991 and was nominated for a Governor General's Award. She publishes regularly in literary magazines in both Canada and abroad and was a guest reader at the Vancouver International Writers' Festival in 1994. Her next book of poetry, tentatively entitled *Darkening In*, will be published by Véhicule Press in 1997.

Esta Spalding was raised in Hawaii and Toronto. She is the author of *Carrying Place* (House of Anansi Press, 1995) and winner of the 1995 Malahat Long Poem Contest. She is the assistant editor of *Brick, A Literary Journal*, and teaches at the University of Guelph. She has recently completed her second volume of poetry.

R. M. Vaughan sometimes lives in Toronto and sometimes in his native New Brunswick, where he was born in 1965. Vaughan was the 1994–1995 Playwright-in-Residence at Buddies in Bad Times Theatre, where seven of his twelve staged plays have been produced. His poems, stories, and essays have appeared in numerous periodicals and anthologies. Vaughan's first solo book of poems, *a selection of dazzling scarves*, will be published by ECW Press in September 1996.

Born in 1951 in Montreal, **Eddy Yanofsky** moved to Toronto in 1981. He is a poet and short story writer, and his first collection of poetry, *In Separate Rooms*, was a chapbook published by Gesture Press in 1990. He won the first Gwendolyn MacEwen Memorial Award for New Canadian Poets in 1991, and works at the University of Toronto Bookstore where he is one of the programmers of its renowned reading series.

AFTERWORD

WE WERE THRILLED when House of Anansi Press approached Beat the Street and asked us to be part of this project to publish new poetry by Toronto writers. Poetry is something we can all share in, and our students in particular find in it a way of freeing their own feelings and experiences:

"Poetry makes you think; it's a way to express facts in a different way, a way to express spiritual thoughts" (BTS student);

"I write poetry all the time. It's easier to express myself through a poem than sitting and talking to someone. You can send a clearer message sometimes through poetry" (BTS peer tutor).

BTS is a downtown literacy centre that works with homeless and marginally housed youth and adults. It was started eleven years ago by two Frontier College learners who had had lots of street experience and knew that literacy is a key to getting off the streets. Their idea, with the help of Frontier College, was to take literacy to the streets, in parks, in coffee shops, in hostels and community centres — an innovative idea.

Today, we still reach out to many people on the street offering them the chance to get back on their feet — and to stay on their feet — by helping them build skills for participation in society. Along with developing literacy skills, we help our students with housing, employment, income, and basic life needs. The programs at BTS run by staff, peer, and community volunteers work collectively to aid students in the struggle to overcome some of the barriers to getting off the street.

Encouraging self-expression through the sharing of poetry and stories is the touchstone of our work together, in small groups and one-to-one. Annually we publish student writings and artwork in a journal called *Heartbeats*. Through literacy and reading we celebrate the successes of young people who come to BTS all too often battered and hungry, isolated, confused, and mistrustful. BTS and the wonder of the word provide a place for rediscovered voices and new voices alike. We are proud to be connecting our poets with the Toronto poets featured in this volume.

— SHAWN CONWAY
Beat the Street

ACKNOWLEDGEMENTS

Christian Bök: "Crystals," "Crystal Lattice," "Figure 2.1," "Emerald," "*from* Diamonds," "Glass," and "Grain Boundaries" were previously published in *Crystallography* (Coach House Press, 1994). Versions of some of the other poems have appeared in the following journals: *Torque*, *Chicago Review*, *Poetry Canada Review*.

Kevin Connolly: "They Remain Hatless," "Junkmale," "Raw Dough," "Arbitrary Cultures," and "Progress Report" were previously published in *Asphalt Cigar* (Coach House Press, 1995). "Order Picker" was included in the anthology *The Last Word* edited by Michael Holmes (Insomniac, 1995). Earlier versions of "Angel Food Cake," "Stop Pulling My Hair," and "Hurtin' Song" appeared in *Who Torched Rancho Diablo*. "Face" is adapted from a poem first published in the chapbook *Pterodactyls* (Pink Dog, 1988).

Laura Lush: "The First Awakening of Summer," "The Other Side of the Lake," "This Farm Where Nothing Sleeps and Nothing Is Invisible," "The Worm Girl," "The Missing Child," "In the Bus Depot," "Jessie," "157 Islington," "In the Puszcza," "After the Monsoon," and "When They Go" first appeared in *Hometown* (Véhicule, 1991).

Esta Spalding: "When the Box Arrived" was published in the journal *Carousel*. The poems "Eggs," "Backyard, Growing Up," "Salt," "Bread," "Then," "Snapshot," "What the Cookbook Doesn't Say," "Moving In," and "Fall" were previously published in *Carrying Place* (House of Anansi Press, 1995).

R. M. Vaughan: "3 poems for Paul Bowles" appeared in the anthology *Plush* (Coach House Press, 1996). Versions of some of the other poems have appeared in the following journals: *Blind Date*, *The Cormorant*, *Element*, *Fiddlehead*, *New Muse of Contempt*, and *Orbus*.

Eddy Yanofsky: "Coat Buttons," "Fragments from the Survival Journal of a Euclid Avenue Resident in the Wilderness," and "Sestina for a Place" originally appeared in *In Separate Rooms* (Gesture Press, 1990).